A Plain & Simple Christmas

Also by Amy Clipston:

A Gift of Grace
A Promise of Hope

A Plain & Simple Christmas

Amy Clipston
Bestselling Author

ZONDERVAN®

ZONDERVAN.com/
AUTHORTRACKER
follow your favorite authors

ZONDERVAN

A Plain and Simple Christmas
Copyright © 2010 by Amy Clipston

This title is also available as a Zondervan ebook.
Visit www.zondervan.com/ebooks.

This title is also available in a Zondervan audio edition.
Visit www.zondervan.fm.

Requests for information should be addressed to:

Zondervan, *Grand Rapids, Michigan 49530*

Library of Congress Cataloging-in-Publication Data

Clipston, Amy.
      A plain and simple Christmas : a novella / Amy Clipston.
         p.   cm.
      ISBN 978-0-310-32736-3
      1. Amish — Fiction. 2. Families — Fiction. 3. Life change events — Fiction. 4.
    Pregnant women — Fiction. 5. Childbirth — Fiction. 6. Christmas stories. I. Title.
    PS3603.L58P58   2010
     813'.6 — dc22
                                                              2010023778

Any Internet addresses (websites, blogs, etc.) and telephone numbers printed in this
book are offered as a resource. They are not intended in any way to be or imply an
endorsement by Zondervan, nor does Zondervan vouch for the content of these sites
and numbers for the life of this book.

Cover design: Thinkpen Design
Cover photography: Shutterstock®, Veer
Interior illustration: iStockphoto
Interior design: Beth Shagene

Printed in the United States of America

---

10 11 12 13 14 15 /DCI/ 21 20 19 18 17 16 15 14 13 12 11 10 9 8 7 6 5 4 3 2 1

With love and appreciation for my godparents,
Joseph and Trudy Janitz.

Uncle Joe — You live on in the precious memories
you left behind.

Aunt Trudy — Thank you for all you do for our family.
We love you!

Glossary

ack: Oh
aenti: aunt
appeditlich: delicious
bedauerlich: sad
boppli: baby
bopplin: babies
bruder: brother
bruderskinner: nieces/nephews
daed: father
danki: Thank you
dat: dad
Dietsch: Pennsylvania Dutch, the Amish
    language (a German dialect)
dochder: daughter
dochdern: daughters
eiferich: excited
Englisher: a non-Amish person
fraa: wife
Frehlicher Grischtdaag!: Merry Christmas!
freind: friend

freinden: friends
freindschaft: relative
froh: happy
gegisch: silly
gern gschehne: You're welcome
grossdaddi: grandfather
grossdochdern: granddaughters
Grischtdaag: Christmas
grossmammi: grandmother
Gude mariye: Good morning
gut: good
Gut nacht: Good night
Ich liebe dich: I love you
kapp: prayer covering or cap
kind: child
kinner: children
kinskind: grandchild
kinskinner: grandchildren
kumm: come
liewe: love, a term of endearment
maedel: young woman
mamm: mom
mei: my
mutter: mother
naerfich: nervous
narrisch: crazy
onkel: uncle
Ordnung: unwritten book of Amish rules

rumspringe: running around time
schee: pretty
schtupp: family room
schweschder: sister
Was iss letz?: What's wrong?
Willkumm heemet: Welcome home
Wie geht's: How do you do? or Good day!
wunderbaar: wonderful
ya: yes

Note to the Reader

While this novel is set against the real backdrop of Lancaster County, Pennsylvania, the characters are fictional. There is no intended resemblance between the characters in this book and any real members of the Amish and Mennonite communities. As with any work of fiction, I've taken license in some areas of research as a means of creating the necessary circumstances for my characters. My research was thorough; however, it would be impossible to be completely accurate in details and description, since each and every community differs. Therefore, any inaccuracies in the Amish and Mennonite lifestyles portrayed in this book are completely due to fictional license.

CHAPTER 1

Anna Mae McDonough closed her eyes and folded her hands across her protruding belly. A tiny bump responded to the touch and she smiled.

"Thank you, Lord, for this bountiful meal on this beautiful Thanksgiving Day," her husband's smooth voice said. "And thank you for all of the blessings we have—our home and our wonderful life together." Kellan paused and Anna Mae glanced up, just as he squeezed her hand.

"Thank you, Lord," Kellan continued, "most of all for our baby who will be here in January. Amen."

"Amen," Anna Mae whispered, squeezing his hand. "Happy Thanksgiving, Kellan."

"Happy Thanksgiving, Annie," he said, his brown eyes filling with warmth.

Butterflies fluttered in her stomach in response to his loving gaze. "It's hard to believe this is our third Thanksgiving in Baltimore."

He filled his plate with slices of turkey and passed her the platter. "Time has flown since I found you in that bakery."

Her smile faded, and she rested her hands on her belly. Memories of Lancaster County crashed down on her.

Holidays spent with her four siblings and their families were chaotic, with children running around the room screaming. Anna Mae would find herself in the kitchen laughing and gossiping with her mother, three sisters, her sister-in-law, and nieces.

Tears filled her eyes as she glanced around her small, empty, quiet house. Kellan's only sister lived clear across the country in Los Angeles. Anna Mae had only met her sister-in-law once, and that was at their wedding three years ago. Kellan's father had died eight years ago, and his mother had abandoned him and his sister when he was ten years old. The only family they had was each other.

And sometimes the silence on holidays was deafening to Anna Mae.

"I'm sorry." Kellan leaned over, taking her hands in his. "I didn't mean to upset you by bringing up Lancaster."

"It's okay," she whispered. She swiped her hand across her wet cheek and forced a smile. "I cherish these times with you and wouldn't give them up for anything." And it was the truth. She'd never for one second regretted leaving her community to build a life with Kellan.

The baby kicked, and she looked down at her belly. Tears clouded her vision as she contemplated her newborn growing up without a host of relatives to love him or her.

"What is it, Annie?" Kellan asked. "I can tell by your expression that you're stewing on something. This delicious dinner is going to get cold if you don't fill your plate soon."

"It's just—" Her voice broke when she met his loving gaze. She cleared her throat and took a deep, ragged breath, hoping to stop the threatening tears. "I have so many memories of holidays and birthdays with my siblings and cousins." She rubbed her belly. "Our baby won't know any of them, and my family won't know our baby."

Kellan frowned and shook his head. "You're upset because it's been so long since you've been together as a family. Maybe after the baby is born, you can see them again."

"Leaning forward, she took his warm hands in hers. "You're probably right, but I wish I could have it all—you *and* my family."

"You can have it all." He shrugged and lifted his glass of Coke. "I've told you I have no objections to seeing your family. You name the time, and we'll go up there and visit them. I can take vacation anytime I want. That's the beauty of being the owner of McDonough Chevrolet. I can take time off and leave it in the hands of my capable staff."

"You know it's not that simple with my father." Despite her sudden loss of appetite, Anna Mae filled her plate with turkey, gravy, stuffing, a homemade roll, and homemade cranberry sauce. Thoughts of her father rolled through her mind. She knew she was at fault for not reaching out more. However, she'd wanted to build a new life without the emotional complications of dealing with the shunning.

"I don't get that whole shunning thing." He shook his head. "They say it's because they love you, but how is cutting off your child showing her you love her?"

"They shun in order to prevent members from leaving the community. When a member leaves, it's emotionally painful for the member's family." With her eyes trained on her plate, she cut some turkey and moved the piece through the gravy. "*Daed's* the bishop for the district, the religious leader. It's his job to keep us on the right path and enforce the rules of the *Ordnung*."

"But we go to our own church. Why isn't that good enough for him and the rest of the community? Why do they have to punish you for leaving?"

Sighing, Anna Mae looked up at him. "Kellan, my family is only following the traditions of the Amish that have come before them. The Amish beliefs and traditions go back a few hundred years. Shunning isn't punishment. They want their children to keep the traditions they've learned from their parents. They respect other Christians and don't believe that other ways of living are wrong. The Amish don't judge others or think their way is the only way. However, they want to keep their children within the community. They love me and want me to come back."

He glowered. "Without me."

She touched his hands. "I'm not going to go back. I just miss my family. I miss seeing them and spending time with them."

Kellan chewed more turkey, his eyes concentrating on his meal. He then looked at her. "How about we go visit them for Christmas? We can just show up and surprise them."

Anna Mae shook her head. "That wouldn't be wise. *Daed* wouldn't take kindly to a surprise visit. I'm certain he loves me, but he's very hurt that I left. I'm sure he thinks I rejected him and my mother."

Kellan's expression brightened. "What if one of your sisters helped you plan it?"

Anna Mae considered his suggestion and then shook her head. "I can't see one of them deliberately going behind my father's back. They'd be sure to tell him before I arrived, and that would make for a very uncomfortable and short visit."

He grinned. "I bet I know someone who would be happy to help you."

"Who?"

"Your brother David's wife."

"Kathryn." Anna Mae nodded, a knot developing in her throat at the thought of her sister-in-law. "She was the most supportive of my relationship with you. She seemed to be the only one in the family who understood why I left. She might consider planning a surprise visit. Kathryn was always known for speaking her mind, despite the consequences."

"Why don't you write her a letter and tell her how you're feeling?"

"Maybe I will." Anna Mae bit her lip, hoping to stop the threatening tears. "I miss her."

"Let's enjoy this delicious meal. After we're done eating, I'll clean up while you write a letter to Kathryn."

"Okay." Anna Mae tried to keep the conversation light while they ate.

After finishing off the meal with pumpkin pie and coffee, Kellan stood and gathered up the dishes. "I'll take care of this. You go write that letter."

"No. Let me help you." Anna Mae rose and reached for his mug.

"Anna Mae," he began with mock annoyance, "I'll take care of the dishes. Go write to Kathryn so you can rest easy tonight. The baby doesn't need the stress you're feeling about your family. Writing to Kathryn will ease your mind."

Stepping around the table, Anna Mae brushed her lips against Kellan's warm cheek. "I don't deserve you."

He set the dishes on the table and swept Anna Mae into his muscular arms. "Actually, I'm the one who doesn't deserve you." He kissed her lips, slow and easy, and then smiled down while brushing back a wisp of light brown hair that had escaped her bun. Even though she now lived an English lifestyle, she always wore her hair up. Some parts of her upbringing were still comfortable to her. "You're so sweet and loyal. I'll never understand how your family could shun you."

"Kellan, I already explained—"

"I know, I know." He held her close and whispered into her ear. "No matter what happens with our family, I love you. Don't forget that."

"I love you too." She closed her eyes, silently thanking God for her wonderful husband.

He let go of the embrace. "Go write your letter. I'll get the dishes under control."

"Thank you." After retrieving her favorite stationery from the roll-top desk, Anna Mae settled into Kellan's easy chair.

At a loss for how to begin the letter, she stared across the room at her favorite wedding portrait of her and Kellan, standing together at the altar of his church. Clad in a simple white dress, Anna Mae stood holding a small bouquet of flowers while clutching Kellan's arm. Her dress and the ceremony were both very different from an Amish wedding, but Anna Mae had wanted to fit into Kellan's English world. After all, she'd broken every Amish rule by leaving her community and marrying him. It was both the happiest and saddest day in her life. Only Kellan's sister and a handful of his friends and employees attended. She'd wished her family would've come, but they had objected to her leaving and did not condone their union. Anna Mae was cut off from the family when she left, even though leaving was her choice.

Closing her eyes, Anna Mae thought back to that fateful day when she'd met Kellan McDonough. It had been four years ago when Kellan had stepped into the Kauffman Amish Bakery in Bird-in-Hand, Pennsylvania, where Anna Mae worked with her sister-in-law Kathryn and Kathryn's relatives.

Anna Mae was twenty-three and had joined the Amish church the previous spring. After a few months of instruction covering the *Ordnung*, the unwritten rules of the Amish, she'd been baptized and had taken a public vow to live by the Amish beliefs. All three of her sisters were married, but Anna Mae had all but given up on finding a mate. She'd been certain she'd become an old maid, working in the bakery and making quilts for auction until she was too old and frail to work.

However, her life had changed irrevocably when a handsome English customer approached her and asked her to sit on the porch with him and share a slice of chocolate cake. Anna Mae hesitated, but Kathryn nudged her forward, telling Anna Mae to relish a much-needed break.

The customer introduced himself as Kellan McDonough, a car dealership owner from Baltimore in town visiting old friends. Kellan's soft-spoken demeanor and easy sense of humor intrigued Anna Mae. She was more comfortable chatting with her new friend than she'd ever felt with the young Amish men in her community.

Their conversation on the porch lasted an hour, ending only when Beth Anne, Kathryn's sister, came looking for Anna Mae. When Kellan said goodbye and shook Anna Mae's hand, a spark ignited between them.

Kellan visited Anna Mae at the bakery every day for the next week and then wrote her letters after he returned to Baltimore. Six months later, he visited her again, and six months after that he proposed to her.

"Annie?" Kellan's concerned voice brought her back to the present. "You all right?"

She opened her eyes and found him standing in the doorway to the kitchen with a pot in one hand and a dishtowel in the other. "Yes, I'm fine," she said. "I was just losing myself in memories."

He dried the pot with the towel. "Good ones, I hope."

She smiled. "The best."

"Do you need anything, like a drink or a snack?"

She groaned. "If I eat anything else, I'll explode. Thank you, though."

"You call me if you need anything."

"I will. Love you." She lifted her pen.

"Love you too." He retreated into the kitchen.

Taking a deep breath, Anna Mae began to write. Once she completed the letter, she signed and sealed it. After addressing the envelope, she closed her eyes and whispered a prayer, asking God to somehow reunite her with her family for Christmas.

CHAPTER 2

Walking up her long driveway, Kathryn Beiler smiled as her middle daughters prattled on about their day at school.

"Naomi told Millie that Danny likes her, but really Danny likes Rebecca," Lizzie said.

"But I heard that Rebecca likes Johnny, and so I—" Ruthie chimed in.

"Will you two take a breath?" Amanda snapped. "You've been yakking ever since you got home. I'm getting a headache." At the age of fourteen, she was Kathryn's oldest child and had already graduated from eighth grade. She now helped out at the bakery with Kathryn.

"Girls," Kathryn said, trying to suppress a laugh. "There's no need for bickering."

Kathryn's two boys, David Jr. and Manny, pushed each other and she gave them a stern warning look before glancing at the stack of envelopes in Amanda's hands. "Did you grab the mail from the box?"

"*Ya, Mamm.*" Amanda gave her the stack. "I think it's mostly bills, but I saw a letter mixed in with them. Looks like it's from Baltimore. Who do we know in Baltimore?"

"Baltimore?" Kathryn wracked her brain. "I'm not certain." Examining the letters, she gasped when she read the return address—*McDonough*.

"What is it, *Mamm*?" Amanda asked, craning her neck to read the envelope.

"Just an old friend." Kathryn shoved the envelopes into the pocket of her apron as she stepped into the foyer. She nodded toward the kitchen. "Boys, please set the table. Girls, you can start on supper. The stew is prepared in the refrigerator. Your *dat* will be home shortly."

While the children tended to supper, Kathryn slipped into the family room, dropping her bag and the stack of letters onto the sofa. She sank into her husband's favorite chair and opened the envelope from Baltimore. Tears filled her eyes as she read the beautiful script written by her youngest sister-in-law.

Dear Kathryn,

I'm sure you're wondering why you're receiving this letter since you only expect a Christmas card from me. However, this year I'm hoping you'll receive more than a card.

I've been thinking about you a lot lately. Actually, I've been thinking of you, my brother, my parents, and the rest of our family. I feel as if I have a hole in my heart since I no longer have everyone in my life. While I know it was my decision to leave the community, it wasn't my decision to be cut off from my family.

Although I'm no longer Amish, Kellan and I are living a Christian life together. However, I would like to

*come back to visit and be a part of the family. Kellan's
only family is his sister who lives in California, and
we haven't seen her since our wedding three years ago.
Without an extended family, the holidays are too quiet in
our little house. I miss the chaos of our Beiler gatherings.
Also, Kellan and I have exciting news to share: we're
expecting our first child in January, and we want our
baby to know my family.*

    *I know it's a lot to ask, but would you please help me
find a way to see the family this Christmas? Kellan and
I would love to travel to Lancaster County and share
the Christmas meal with you, David, and the rest of the
Beiler family. You were the only one who understood why
I left, so I know you could convince the rest of the family
that I want to be a part of Christmas this year.*

    *Please consider my idea and write me back. Even if
you don't think it's a possibility for us to visit, would you
please let me know how everyone is? How are my parents
doing? Does my father ever speak of me?*

    I look forward to hearing from you soon.

*Blessings to you and your family,
Anna Mae*

Kathryn read the letter three times with tears trickling
down her cheeks. Memories swirled through her mind. Anna
Mae was going to be a mother! What a blessing. Oh, how she
missed her sister-in-law!

"*Aenti* Anna Mae," a voice said.

Kathryn's eyes cut to the doorway where Amanda stood,
her arms folded across her thin frame and her blue eyes confident. "That letter is from *Aenti* Anna Mae," Amanda said.

Kathryn nodded. "*Ya.*"

Amanda lowered herself into the chair across from her. "What does it say?"

Kathryn paused, considering if she should share the letter or not. She knew the contents might upset David, since he'd felt caught between his father and Anna Mae when she'd decided to leave. However, Amanda was old enough to understand the situation, giving Kathryn no reason to distrust her.

"If I tell you," Kathryn began, "you must promise to keep this to yourself, Amanda. Your *dat* may not be happy when he finds out."

"So you're going to keep it from him?" Her brow furrowed with disapproval. "Is that the right thing to do?"

Kathryn smiled, both proud of her daughter's honesty and embarrassed by her own perceived dishonesty. "You're right. It's not right for me to keep this from your *dat*, but I need to figure out the best time to tell him. It's up to me to decide when to tell him, not you. Understand?"

"*Ya.*" Her daughter shrugged. "I don't understand why it should matter, but I promise not to share it with anyone."

"Anna Mae and her husband want to visit for Christmas."

Amanda grinned. "That's *wunderbaar*! We haven't seen *Aenti* Anna Mae for three years. Manny was just a baby when she left."

"Shhh," Kathryn hissed. "You can't say it too loud. If Lizzie or Ruthie overhear, you know what will happen."

Amanda rolled her eyes. "The whole district will know by tomorrow morning."

Kathryn clicked her tongue. "Now, now, you were just like them when you were around eleven."

"I doubt that," Amanda muttered. Her expression brightened. "Back to the letter. What exactly did she say?"

"She asked if I would help her plan a visit for Christmas. She and her husband are expecting a baby in January and they want the family to know their baby. It sounds like a *wunderbaar* idea, but your *Grossdaddi* Beiler won't be as open to it as we are."

"Because *Aenti* Anna Mae was shunned for leaving and marrying an Englisher."

"That's exactly right." Kathryn folded the letter and slipped it into the envelope.

Amanda shook her head, and the ties on her prayer *kapp* fluttered around her neck. "It's sad. She should be allowed to come for Christmas."

"She can visit, but your *grossdaddi* won't be as welcoming as the rest of us. It will be uncomfortable at best."

The back door opened and banged shut, followed by a chorus of children's voices yelling, "*Dat!*"

Kathryn dropped the letter into the pocket of her apron and gave Amanda a hard look. "Remember, this is our secret, *ya*?"

Winking, Amanda stood. "What letter? I have no idea what you're talking about."

Kathryn shook her head and swallowed a chuckle. She hoped the ease of her daughter's fib wasn't a glimpse into the future of her approaching *rumspringe*. She followed Amanda into the kitchen, where David stood surrounded by his children, smiling and nodding while they shared the details of their day.

He turned his gaze to Kathryn and his smile deepened,

causing her heart to warm. His smile still thrilled her, even after fifteen years of marriage.

She smiled in return and rested her hands on her apron, silently debating her choice to conceal the letter.

The children continued chatting, and David nodded while moving past them to the doorway. "*Wie geht's?*" he whispered, before brushing his lips across hers.

"*Gut,*" she said. "How are you?"

"Tired." He removed his hat and hung it on a peg on the wall. He brushed back his sandy blond hair, which was matted from the hat.

Kathryn crossed the kitchen and checked the stew on the stove. "It looks like supper is ready. Everyone go wash up."

The children filed out of the kitchen, chattering away in Pennsylvania *Dietsch* as Kathryn stirred the stew, savoring the aroma.

"How was your day?" she asked.

"*Gut.* The store was busy, which always makes my father happy. People always need farming supplies, no matter the time of year or the weather." He leaned over the pot. "Stew?"

"*Ya.*" She continued to stir it. "Your favorite."

"*Danki.*" He inhaled a deep breath. "Smells *appeditlich.* How was your day?"

"*Gut,*" she said. "The English customers love to come into the bakery this time of year and get desserts for their Christmas parties. We were busy all day long."

David snatched a spoon from the counter and sampled the stew. "Like I said, *appeditlich.* You make the best stew in Lancaster County."

She smiled. "You tend to exaggerate."

"No, I don't." He dropped the spoon into the sink and then moved behind her.

Hands encircled her waist, and she yelped. Looking up behind her, she found David leaning down. His lips brushed her neck, and she giggled while shivers danced up her spine.

"What has gotten into you, David Beiler?" she asked, placing her hands on his.

He turned her toward him and pulled her into a warm hug. "Isn't a man allowed to miss his *fraa*?" He leaned down to kiss her again, and then stopped when gagging noises erupted across the room.

Kathryn glanced over to her older son, David Jr., holding his neck while feigning to choke. His siblings surrounded him, and giggles erupted among the group of five children.

"I guess we'll have to continue this later," Kathryn whispered to David with a grin.

"*Ya*, I suppose so." David stepped over to the sink and washed his hands, while Kathryn and the children brought the food to the table.

Kathryn sat at the table surrounded by her children and across from her husband. When they all bowed their heads in silent prayer, she thanked God for the bountiful blessings in her life, including her family.

Then she sent up a special prayer, asking God to lead her toward a solution to making Anna Mae and her husband welcome for Christmas.

❧

The following morning, Kathryn stood in the doorway separating the kitchen from the front of the bakery and observed her mother straightening the counter, placing sample containers in a row, and humming her favorite hymn.

She glanced behind her at her sister Beth Anne and daughter Amanda chatting while icing a chocolate cake.

Spotting no customers in the bakery, Kathryn sidled up to her mother. "Can I help you?" she asked.

"No, *danki*, I think that about covers it." Elizabeth stood up straight. "I believe the cakes and cookies are well stocked. It may be just as busy today as it was yesterday."

"*Ya*. I was telling David just last night how busy we've been." Kathryn placed her hand on her apron.

Elizabeth's eyes filled with concern. "What's on your mind, Kathryn? You look like the weight of the world is sitting on your shoulders."

Kathryn pulled the letter from her pocket. "I received this yesterday."

Elizabeth took the letter and read it. "Anna Mae is pregnant. What a blessing! And she wants to come and visit." She smiled. "What did David say about it?"

"I didn't tell him." Kathryn busied herself by straightening a row of individually wrapped cookies to avoid her *mamm's* stunned stare.

"Why not?" Elizabeth chuckled. "You're never one to keep silent about things. What's stopping you this time?"

Sighing, Kathryn looked up. "I know he'll think it's a bad idea to invite Anna Mae. He'll say her visit will open family wounds that he wants kept closed. You know how his *dat* gets about this subject."

Amanda appeared in the doorway. "But it's *Grischtdaag*! *Aenti* Anna Mae is our family, and the holidays are about family. Jesus tells us to love one another and forgive each other. *Grossdaddi* needs to remember that."

"He knows that, Amanda," Kathryn said. "You know as well as I do that he preaches about love and forgiveness, but he's in a complicated position because he's the bishop."

"But it's *Grischtdaag, Mamm*," Amanda repeated with more emphasis on the word. "Can't our family put the shunning behind us for that?" Amanda's face transformed to her best "puppy dog face," as her father called it. "Please, *Mamm*. Please."

Grimacing, Kathryn glanced at her mother, who cupped her hand to her mouth and chuckled.

Kathryn turned back to her daughter. "Fine. You win. I'll talk to your *dat*, but I can't make any promises about what will happen."

Amanda squealed and threw her arms around Kathryn's neck, jerking her into a hug.

"You're the master of manipulation, Amanda Joy," Kathryn said, hugging her daughter close. "I feel sorry for the boys in our community when you start courting."

Amanda giggled and then danced back into the kitchen.

Kathryn shook her head. "She's a handful."

"*Ya*," Elizabeth said, looping an arm around Kathryn's shoulder. "She reminds me of you at that age. You knew how to get just what you wanted too." Her expression became serious. "You're doing the right thing by discussing it with David. Tell him how you feel and how much more complete *Grischtdaag* will be with his youngest *schweschder* back with the family."

"I just hope he'll listen," Kathryn whispered.

"He loves you." Elizabeth patted her back. "He'll listen."

That evening Kathryn ran a brush through her waist-length golden hair while watching David lounge on the bed reading his Bible.

"I can feel your stare," he said without looking up. "What's on your mind, Katie?"

She cleared her throat and set the brush on the dresser her father had made as a wedding gift for her and David years ago. "I wanted to share something with you."

David closed the Bible and set it on the night table. "What is it?"

She plucked Anna Mae's letter from the dresser and handed it to him. "Please read this with an open heart and mind."

He raised his eyebrows in curiosity and took the letter. Kathryn held her breath while David scanned it.

Sighing, he glanced up and handed the paper back to her. "You know as well as I do that this would be a bad idea."

"But she's your *schweschder*, David. She's family. Isn't *Grischtdaag* about celebrating the birth of our Savior as a family?"

"She left the faith. As my father said, she made her choice." He lifted his Bible and flipped it open.

She placed the letter on the bureau and then climbed under the quilts next to him in the bed. "David, there's no harm in her visiting."

David closed the Bible and set it on his nightstand before facing her. A frown creased his handsome face and forehead. "I don't have to tell you that it's much more complicated than a simple visit. None of your siblings left the community, so you have no idea how it affected our family."

"That's not fair," Kathryn said with a frown. "I was here when she left. I saw how much it hurt us all. You know I love her like I love my own sisters."

"You're right. That wasn't a fair statement for me to make." He sighed. "I'm sorry. Her leaving was very painful for my parents. It's as if she became a stranger to my parents. She's no longer following our traditions. You know that if she came to visit, my father would be very upset."

"But it's been three years. Isn't it time for the family to heal? Life is so short. We saw that firsthand when my sister Sarah lost her husband in the fire at the furniture store. We never know when the Lord may call us home." She gave him her best pleading look, the one that usually got him to change his mind. "We had a lot of fun working together at the bakery. When she left, she also left a void in my life and a hole in my heart. I'm sure you feel the same way and miss her too."

"Of course I miss her." He snuggled down under the covers and pulled Kathryn close. "Let's not argue about this, Katie. You know that it's not a good idea to invite my sister for *Grischtdaag*. Maybe we can take the *kinner* and see her in the spring. We could take the train down. The *kinner* would love it."

Kathryn inhaled his comforting scent, soap mixed with his spicy deodorant. "*Ya*, they would love it." *But it's not the same as Grischtdaag!*

"We'll plan a trip," he said, his voice softening. "In the spring. *Ya*, it will be *gut*, and it won't involve my father and his temper."

She nodded, though she wasn't convinced waiting until the spring would help heal the family. She listened to his breathing as it changed, slowing down and deepening. Her mind swirled with ideas of how she could arrange to invite Anna Mae without alienating David. Surely he would change his mind when his sister was standing in front of him.

Although she was going against her husband's wishes, she couldn't shake the feeling that it was God's will for Anna Mae to come and see the family again.

Kathryn's thoughts turned to the time of Anna Mae's decision to leave the community. Oh, how Mary Rose, Anna Mae's mother, had cried. Mary Rose had begged Anna Mae to stay, promising that Anna Mae would find a nice Amish man to marry. However, Anna Mae had insisted that Kellan was the love of her life and she was meant to marry him.

Mary Rose had taken to her bed for a week after Anna Mae left. She'd said that the pain of seeing her daughter leave had debilitated her.

Wouldn't it be God's will for Mary Rose to see her daughter again and know that she was well and happy with her English husband?

Kathryn waited until she was certain David was in a deep sleep and then she wiggled out of his grasp, gingerly rose from the bed, and plucked the letter from the bureau. She took the kerosene lamp from the nightstand, lit it, and tiptoed down to the kitchen.

She fished her stationery from the desk and sat at the table. Closing her eyes, she sent up a silent prayer for the right words. She then poised her pen and began to write a letter to Anna Mae.

CHAPTER 3

Opening the mailbox, Anna Mae fished out a stack of envelopes from inside and leafed through them.

"Bills, bills, bills," she mumbled with a sigh. They always came near the first of the month. But when Anna Mae came to a plain white envelope with pretty penmanship, her heart fluttered. She read the return address, squealed with delight, and hugged the envelope to her chest.

Kathryn had answered!

Anna Mae rushed into the house, dropped her bag on the kitchen table, and tore the envelope open. Lowering herself into a chair, she read the letter.

Dear Anna Mae,

I was overjoyed to receive your letter. It seems like only yesterday that you were with my sisters and me in the bakery, making cookies and cakes while laughing and sharing stories about our friends in the community.

How wunderbaar that God will soon bless you with your first baby! You and Kellan must be overjoyed! I'm so very happy for you and will keep you and your baby in my prayers.

My mamm, sisters, nieces, and I stay busy these days. The bakery is very busy right now during the holidays, and we're still a favorite tourist stop during the spring, summer, and fall.

The family is all doing well. Amanda is fourteen, Ruthie is twelve, Lizzie is ten, Junior is eight, and Manny is four. David says he wants more, but we'll have to wait and see what the Lord has in store for us. Your mamm and dat are in good health, as are your siblings, nieces, and nephews. Our family is very blessed.

It would be wunderbaar to have you and Kellan come for Grischtdaag! I can't think of a better time of year for the family to reunite. Would you like me to work out the details for you? How many days would you and Kellan like to stay? Do you know where you'd like to stay? Of course, you're welcome to stay with us, but you might be more comfortable at the Paradise Bed and Breakfast. Perhaps you'd like to stay there instead?

I look forward to hearing from you soon.

> *God's blessing to you and your family,*
> *Kathryn*

Anna Mae read and reread the letter until she'd nearly committed it to memory. Tears spilled from her eyes while she remembered the time she'd spent at the bakery with Kathryn, Kathryn's sisters, her nieces, and Kathryn's *mamm*, Elizabeth. Those were some of the best memories she cherished from Lancaster County.

Glancing at the clock, Anna Mae realized Kellan would be home for supper in an hour. She folded the letter and put it back into the envelope and then into the pocket of her sweater. She then hoisted herself from the chair, headed to the refrigerator, and rooted around until she found a pack of steaks, Kellan's favorite. After marinating the steaks in his favorite barbeque sauce, she placed them in the oven set to broil and stuck a couple of potatoes in the microwave.

Anna Mae was preparing a green salad when Kellan entered the kitchen clad in one of his best suits.

"How was your day?" he asked before kissing her cheek. Leaning down, he cupped his hand to her belly. "And how was your day, Lug Nut?"

"Lug Nut? How can you be so sure it's a boy?" she asked with a chuckle.

He shrugged. "Just a hunch."

She smiled, rubbing her belly. "We had a good day. The quilting circle at church was a lot of fun. We caught each other up on the latest church news and also got a lot accomplished for our quilt drive. How was your day?"

"It was good. Busy. Sales have gone up this month, which makes everyone at the dealership happy." He breathed in the aroma emanating from the stove and moaned. "Steak?" He eyed her with suspicion. "What are you up to, Annie?"

"Nothing." She gave him her best innocent smile and carried the salad bowl to the table. "I thought you might like to have your favorite tonight."

His lips curled into a grin. "Is that so?" He retrieved plates and utensils and set the table. "You seem to be scheming over something. I know when you're fibbing. Steak is always an ulterior motive for something."

"Maybe I prepared your favorite meal because I love you."

Anna Mae brought the steak and potatoes to the table while Kellan gathered the condiments and glasses of water for them.

After saying grace, they began to eat.

"I can tell by the expression on your pretty face that you're excited to share something with me," he said, cutting up his steak. "What's up?"

"I've been dying to tell you. I have good news!" Anna Mae fished the letter from her pocket. "I received this today."

While he read the letter, she smiled, thinking of her upcoming trip to Lancaster County at Christmas. A bump on her belly drew her attention to the unborn baby. She rested her hand on her abdomen and smiled while rubbing the location of the movement. She longed to give her child the gift of knowing her family in Lancaster. The trip was for her baby and the baby's future as a member of the Beiler family.

Kellan looked up and placed the letter on the table beside his plate. His expression was cautious. "I guess this means you want to go to Lancaster for Christmas. That's what *Grischtdaag* is, right? Christmas?"

"Yes, that's right. *Grischtdaag* is Christmas." Anna Mae nodded toward her belly. "I want to do this for our baby. Now is the best time to try to make amends."

He gave a tentative smile. "It sounds like a great idea, but I want you to be sure this is what you want. I don't want you to get hurt. Your father used some harsh words when you left. I'll never forget his words to you, Annie. He said you were no longer his daughter if you left."

She moved her hand over her abdomen in response to more kicks. "He didn't mean that. He said it out of anger, hurt, and disappointment. I was his only child to leave the faith and the community."

Kellan's eyes moved to her belly and a smile curved his lips. "Is he moving?"

She nodded. "I think *she's* doing somersaults." She gave a grin.

"I bet my boy likes steak. He's a chip off the old block." He placed his hand on her belly, and she covered it with her hand. "Wow." His grin widened as he met her gaze. "He does like steak. He's telling you to make it more often, Mommy."

"Yes, maybe she does like steak, Daddy. Girls can like steak too." Leaning over, she brushed her lips against his.

"I love you," he said, his smile fading. "That's why I support this trip, but I also don't want your family to hurt you—especially now."

"But you encouraged me to write the letter. Why are you changing your mind?"

"I thought about it more and I keep remembering how your father behaved when you left. I'm nervous about it." He nodded toward her belly. "Your family could get you upset and then something could happen to him or her." He shook his head, frowning. "Maybe we should wait until the summer or even next fall. By then the baby will be older, and traveling will be easier for us. If we wait, then we don't have to risk you getting upset and something happening to you or the baby."

"I doubt anything bad will happen. I have a good feeling that this trip will go well, and I'll get my family back." She lifted his hands and intertwined her fingers with his. "Please don't change your mind about this. It's really important to me. Please do this for me. Let me see my family and try to rebuild a relationship with them."

He sighed, brushing back a lock of her hair with the fingers of his free hand. "Tomorrow you see the doctor, and you can get her opinion. If she says it's safe for you to travel, then I'll go to make you happy. But if your family upsets you, then I'll bring you home immediately."

"It's a deal." She kissed his cheek. "Thank you. If the doctor says it's safe, then I'll call Kathryn and see what I can arrange."

"I need you to make me one promise, though." He grimaced. "Just don't make me stay at your father's house."

She laughed. "I promise I won't."

Kathryn handed the customer her change and her bag of pastries. "Thank you. Have a nice day."

As the woman walked toward the door, the bakery phone began to ring. Kathryn picked up the phone and cradled it between her ear and her neck.

"Good afternoon," she said. "Kauffman Amish Bakery."

"Hello," a hesitant voice said. "May I please speak with Kathryn?"

"This is she." Kathryn absently straightened packages of cookies on the counter. "How may I help you?"

"Kathryn," the voice said. "This is Anna Mae."

Kathryn gasped and sank onto a stool behind her. "Oh my goodness! Anna Mae! *Wie geht's?*"

"I'm doing pretty well," Anna Mae said. "How are you?"

"*Gut.*" Kathryn glanced across the bakery showroom, glad

to find it empty of customers. "I was so glad to hear from you. Congratulations on your baby!"

"Thank you. I was delighted that you answered. I'm glad everyone is well." She paused, as if gathering her thoughts. "Has my father asked about me or mentioned me at all?"

Kathryn bit her lip, debating what to say. She didn't want to lie, but the truth wouldn't be easy to swallow.

"It's okay," Anna Mae said quickly. "I didn't think he had. You don't need to smooth it over."

"I'm sorry," Kathryn said. "I wish I had better news about him, but no, he hasn't said anything to me. He may have said something to David."

"I doubt it. How's my *mamm*?"

"She's *gut*." Kathryn fingered her apron while she spoke. "She splits her time between helping care for her *kinskinner* and working in the farm store."

Anna Mae sniffed. "I'm so glad to hear it." Her voice quavered, and she cleared her throat. "I'm glad your *kinner* are doing well. I bet they're all getting so big."

"*Ya*." Kathryn chuckled. "David wants ten. I'm leaving it in the Lord's hands."

Anna Mae asked about her three sisters, and Kathryn gave her an update on their lives.

"So much has changed in three years," Anna Mae said. "I feel like I've been gone for a lifetime."

"It hasn't been that long." Kathryn glanced at the doorway and found her mother watching her with a smile. "Are you and Kellan still considering coming for *Grischtdaag*?"

"I saw my doctor yesterday, and she said that it's safe for

me to travel. So, I really want to come." Her voice was small, unsure.

Kathryn paused, considering her husband's disapproval. Still, Kathryn believed it was God's will for the family to heal. "Do you want me to work out the details for you?" she asked, the words flowing despite her hesitation.

"Yes, please."

Kathryn ran her fingers over the edge of the counter. "When will you arrive?"

"The Wednesday before Christmas."

"That sounds perfect." Kathryn found a notepad and pen by the phone. "Give me your phone number so we can keep in touch." She wrote down the number as Anna Mae rattled it off. "I'll see what I can arrange."

"*Danki*." Anna Mae's voice shook again. "It means more than you know."

They chatted about the weather and then hung up. Standing, Kathryn turned and found Amanda and her mother with expectant expressions.

"I guess that was *Aenti* Anna Mae?" Amanda asked.

"*Ya*, it was." Kathryn sat back on the stool.

"And she's coming for *Grischtdaag*?" Amanda clasped her hands together, her eyes glistening with hope.

"She wants to come." Kathryn glanced at Elizabeth, hoping for an answer, a reason to go against David's wishes.

Elizabeth's eyes assessed her. "And you think it's a bad idea?"

Kathryn blew out a frustrated sigh. "David is against it."

"What?" Amanda gasped. "*Dat* doesn't want to see *Aenti* Anna Mae? Why?"

"It's complicated, Amanda," Kathryn said, folding her hands over her apron. "We've already discussed this."

"*Grossdaddi* will understand," Amanda said. "He'll welcome her back and the family will all be together again." Amanda looked between Kathryn and Elizabeth. "Besides, everyone is happy when someone is expecting a baby. *Grossdaddi* will be so happy to see her that he'll forget all about how disappointed he was when she left."

Elizabeth looped her arm around Amanda and pulled her into a hug. "You're such a smart *maedel*."

Kathryn studied her mother's eyes. "So you would go against *Dat* if you believed something in your heart?"

Elizabeth shrugged. "Depending upon the circumstance, maybe."

"And in this circumstance?" Amanda asked.

Elizabeth winked. "One of my English customers once said it's easier to ask for forgiveness than to get permission."

Kathryn glanced at Amanda. "Don't say anything to your siblings or *Dat*. I need to figure this out by myself before your *dat* finds out about it."

"But is that right, *Mamm*?" Amanda folded her arms and frowned. "Shouldn't *Dat* know about this? *Aenti* Anna Mae is his *schweschder*."

Kathryn gave Amanda a stern look.

Amanda sighed. "Fine. My lips are sealed," she grumbled and marched back into the kitchen.

"What am I teaching *mei dochder*?" Kathryn muttered, rubbing her temple.

Elizabeth touched her arm. "You're teaching her to follow her heart when she feels God speaking to her. If Anna Mae is meant to come here, then the plans will fall together and all will work out the way God wants it to."

Kathryn shook her head and grimaced. "I pray you're right."

Later that evening, Kathryn placed the last clean dish in the cabinet and thanked the girls for helping clean up after supper. The girls ran upstairs to take their baths and get ready for bed.

The back door opened and slammed, and David entered the kitchen and sighed. "Chores are done. It's been a long day," he said, sitting at the kitchen table. "It feels good to relax."

"*Ya*," she whispered. She grabbed two glasses of water and sat across from him. Thoughts swirled through her mind like a tornado. Guilt weighed down on her, feeling like a stone sitting on her chest and stealing her breath. How could she possibly deceive the man who'd been her best friend and confidante since she was a child?

"Is something wrong, Katie?" he asked, lifting his glass. "You seem preoccupied." He took a long drink.

Kathryn cleared her throat. "I spoke to Anna Mae today."

His eyes widened with shock. "You spoke to her? What do you mean?"

She took a sip of water and cleared her throat. "She called the bakery."

"How is she?"

"She's doing *gut*." She traced the condensation on the glass with her fingertip. "She and Kellan still want to come and visit for *Grischtdaag*. I told her it sounded like a nice idea." She inhaled a breath, awaiting his response.

"Katie." Reaching over, he took her hand in his. "You know it's a bad idea. I told you we'll go visit her in the spring, and that's what we'll do. Forget any plans for their coming for *Grischtdaag*. It just won't work out the way you'd like."

"But David, it's *Grischtdaag*. The family should be together."

"You know as well as I do that having Anna Mae and her husband here would just upset my *dat*. We don't want that at *Grischtdaag*. We'll go to Baltimore and visit Anna Mae in the spring and discuss inviting her back another time. We'll have to warn my *daed* about it and prepare for the visit. Having them just drop in would cause problems that I'm not ready to face."

"But I really feel that this is the time to invite her," she said slowly, choosing her words as best she could. "It feels like God is leading me to this. I feel it strongly in my heart, David. I'm not just making this decision lightly. It's coming from the very depths of my soul."

"I'm too tired to discuss this now, Katie." He yawned. "The store was busy all day long, and I'm ready to read the Bible and relax. We'll go see my *schweschder* in the spring. That's it. It's decided." He stood. "This discussion is over." He started for the door.

"Wait." Kathryn stood and took a deep breath. "I'm not finished."

Turning, he raised his eyebrows.

"You read the letter," she said. "Anna Mae and Kellan are expecting their first child. They want to rebuild their relationship with the family for the child's sake." She stepped over to him. "Surely you can understand that."

He frowned. "I've already told you that we'll visit her in the spring. You need to let this go. A Christmas visit is not a good idea. There's nothing else to discuss."

"But David—"

He grimaced. "There's nothing else to discuss, Kathryn." He turned and crossed the room, and Kathryn's resentment simmered in her soul.

Glowering, she snatched the glasses from the table and washed them. David had a knack for deciding when a discussion was over, whether she was finished making her case or not. David had no problem walking away when they'd had a heated debate. He would let it go, not discussing it any further. He would probably be reticent the rest of the evening, but by tomorrow he'd be past it, acting as if the disagreement had never happened. However, Kathryn would hang onto her resentment, mulling the problem over and over again in her mind and thinking of everything she should've said to him to make her case.

She knew tonight would be one of those nights when she'd go to bed and lie awake for hours, probably most of the night. While drying the glasses, she contemplated Anna Mae. Kathryn's heart had swelled at the sound of Anna Mae's voice. She had sounded so hopeful on the phone, so desperate to be reunited with her family.

How could a family reunion at Christmastime be wrong? Wasn't that the best time of year for a family to work out issues and become one again? Besides, Anna Mae was building bridges for her unborn child. Surely David understood that!

David's concern regarding his father's temper was valid. Henry Beiler was a strict bishop who stuck to the rules and expected the district, especially his family, to follow suit.

While Henry was a stickler for the Amish way, he also had a big heart. She'd seen him drop whatever he was doing to help a family in need. He'd organized more than one barn raising, and he had also spent long hours helping Kathryn's father and brothers rebuild the furniture store after it burned down. Kathryn loved and respected her father-in-law, and she believed that deep down he missed his youngest daughter and would be overjoyed to see her come back at Christmas. Why couldn't David see that?

Kathryn placed the clean glasses into the cabinet and squeezed her eyes shut. She wished she knew the right answer. Was inviting Anna Mae to Christmas against her husband's wishes a mistake? Was it a sin to make the plans behind her husband's back? Of course it was, since she'd have to lie to David in order to arrange for Anna Mae to come. Lying was always a sin.

But was not revealing the whole truth a lie?

She rubbed her temples. Of course it was a lie. She'd punished her children more than once for leaving out important details in their stories, telling them they'd lied.

Kathryn folded her hands. She needed a sign. She needed God to reveal the right answer to her.

Gnawing her lower lip, she sent up a silent prayer to God, asking—no pleading with Him—for a sign, a clear-cut sign, that inviting Anna Mae was the right decision for the Beiler family's Christmas.

CHAPTER 4

Saturday morning, Kathryn wiped down the counter in the large, open bakery kitchen. When a flurry of Pennsylvania *Dietsch* floated in from the front of the store, she moved to the doorway and found her mother-in-law, Mary Rose, chatting with her mother and Amanda.

Kathryn approached Mary Rose and hugged her. "*Wie geht's?*"

"*Gut.*" Mary Rose smiled. "How are you?"

"*Gut.* What brings you out here?" Kathryn asked.

"I wanted to see how you all were doing." She glanced toward Elizabeth. "David told me the bakery has been hectic with Englishers coming in for goodies for their Christmas parties. I'm glad to hear the bakery is staying so busy."

"*Ya,* it has been busy. You've come by during a lull today. We had a rush earlier." Elizabeth gestured toward the kitchen. "Can I get you some coffee and a piece of chocolate cake?"

Mary Rose brightened. "That sounds *wunderbaar. Danki.*"

Elizabeth touched Amanda's arm. "Will you help me?"

"*Ya,*" Amanda said, following her into the kitchen.

Kathryn gestured toward one of the small tables across from the counter. "Let's have a seat. It's nice and quiet now,

47

so we can talk for a while." She led Mary Rose to the table. "How's Henry doing?" she asked as she sat.

"Oh, he's *gut*," Mary Rose said, lowering herself into a chair. "He's been busy at the store. I'm sure David has told you that they've had a nonstop stream of customers the past week."

"*Ya*, he has." Kathryn ran her fingers over the cool wooden table. "I'm glad to hear it."

Mary Rose's gaze focused across the room and her smile faded. "Can I tell you something, Kathryn?"

"Of course. *Was iss letz?*"

"Nothing's wrong, but there's something I want to share with you because I know you'll understand." Mary Rose sighed and looked at Kathryn. "Lately, I can't stop thinking about Anna Mae. I've dreamed of her nearly every night the past week. I can't stop worrying about her."

Kathryn cupped her hand to her mouth to squelch the gasp bubbling up from her throat. Was this the sign from God she'd prayed for?

Mary Rose, unaffected by Kathryn's reaction, kept talking. "I want to know how she is. Is she *froh* with her life with Kellan in Baltimore? Does she need anything? Does she miss us? Does she have any *kinner*? If so, will I ever know them?"

"Have you tried to contact her lately?" Kathryn asked, hoping to conceal her shock at Mary Rose's revelation.

Mary Rose shook her head, tears glistening in her brown eyes. "Not since last *Grischtdaag*. She sends me a card with a short letter every year and I send her one in return."

"Have you ever considered inviting her for *Grischtdaag*?" Kathryn bit her lip, hoping Mary Rose would say yes.

Frowning, Mary Rose shook her head. "Henry wouldn't hear of it."

"But we're permitted to see those who are shunned. You know that."

"You know your father-in-law." Mary Rose's voice quavered, and she cleared her throat and wiped her eyes. "He would only agree to see her if she were coming back to make things right with the church. I believe her love for Kellan is strong and she's left the Amish church for good. I just wish I could see her again. No matter what, she's my *dochder*, and I miss her terribly."

Kathryn traced the wood grain on the table. "What if she came to visit you? How do you think Henry would react?"

Mary Rose's expression was pensive. "If Anna Mae were to come here, Henry would have to face her, wouldn't he?" Her expression fell. "But she won't come. After what Henry said to her, she has no reason to come back."

"Unless she misses you as much as you miss her." Kathryn raised her eyebrows in response to Mary Rose's surprised expression.

Elizabeth sidled up to the table balancing a tray of four cups of coffee with Amanda in tow, holding a tray with a chocolate cake, forks, and napkins. While Amanda set out the cake and place settings, Elizabeth added a mug at each setting.

"Enjoy," Elizabeth said as she sat across from Mary Rose.

Mary Rose forked some chocolate cake into her mouth and moaned. "This is *wunderbaar. Danki*, Elizabeth."

Kathryn ate a moist piece of cake and sipped the coffee while Elizabeth and Mary Rose discussed the weather, their families, and upcoming holidays. Their conversation was only background noise to the thoughts whirling through her mind. Mary Rose's eyes had spoken volumes of the emotions in her soul for Anna Mae—sadness, regret, love, and worry.

Was this the sign from God that Kathryn had been waiting for?

Yes! Absolutely it was!

The answer was right before Kathryn—she needed to arrange for Anna Mae to visit at Christmas. God was giving her the direction, and she needed to let Him use her to heal the Beiler family.

Kathryn tried her best to appear interested in the idle conversation around her, nodding and smiling at the appropriate times. However, internally, she was swallowing her excitement and anticipation. She couldn't wait to call her friends in Paradise and see if their bed and breakfast was available the week of Christmas.

She needed to be discreet with the plans so David didn't find out before Anna Mae arrived. Because if he did . . .

"Kathryn?" a voice asked.

Kathryn looked up and found her mother-in-law's brown eyes studying her.

"Are you okay?" Mary Rose asked.

"*Ya.*" Kathryn cleared her throat, hoping to appear casual. "I was just thinking about everything I have to do before *Grischtdaag.*" In her peripheral vision, Kathryn spotted her mother giving her a skeptical look. Elizabeth was always a master at reading her children's expressions and their true emotions.

"I reckon I'd better be going," Mary Rose said. "*Danki* for a lovely visit and delicious food." She stood and gathered her dirty mug, fork, and napkin.

Amanda rose and took the items from her and set them on the table. "Just leave it, *Grossmammi*. I'll take care of it." She hugged her. "I'm glad you came to see us."

Mary Rose kissed Amanda's head. "Oh, *danki*, Amanda. You're such a sweet *maedel*." Looping her arm around Amanda's shoulders, they started for the door.

Kathryn followed them to the door. "It was *wunderbaar* to see you, *Mamm*. We'll visit you soon." She gave her a quick hug, and while Amanda and Elizabeth said their goodbyes, Kathryn hurried back to the table and loaded a tray with the dirty forks, mugs, and napkins.

Kathryn was washing the mugs and forks when Elizabeth came up behind her.

"What was really on your mind during Mary Rose's visit?" Elizabeth asked.

Wiping her hands on a rag, Kathryn faced her. "I think God spoke to me today."

Elizabeth raised her eyebrows. "When?"

"While you and Amanda were preparing the cake and coffee, Mary Rose spilled her heart to me, telling me how much she's been thinking of Anna Mae and wishing she could see her and know she was doing well."

Elizabeth gasped. "Oh my."

Kathryn dropped the rag on the counter and grasped Elizabeth's sleeves. "This is the sign I prayed for. I asked God to give me a sign that I'm doing the right thing by helping Anna Mae come for a visit. This was the sign, *Mamm*. He answered me, and I'm going to listen."

Elizabeth smiled. "So it seems that God does bless this visit from Anna Mae."

"I guess so," Kathryn said. "Would you walk out front with me?" She led her mother to the front counter. "Do you think I should make a reservation for them at the Paradise B&B so they have privacy? They may want to get away from the family at night and be alone."

Elizabeth nodded and fished the phone book from the pile of papers on the desk. "That's a great idea. I'll find the number for you." She pointed out the number, and Kathryn's heart pounded as she dialed.

While the phone rang, she hoped David would forgive her for going behind his back and that God would lead the family to a joyous reconciliation in honor of His Son's birth.

On Sunday, Kathryn carried a pitcher of water from her sister-in-law Vera Zook's kitchen to the large family room where the rows of tables were set for the noon meal after the church service. Keeping with tradition, the service had been held in the large room with the moveable walls pushed out in order to accommodate the backless benches for the members of the church district. Families within the district took turns hosting the services every other Sunday during the year. A schedule was set up in advance so that each family would know when it was their turn.

After the four-hour service, the benches were transformed into tables, and the women retired to the kitchen to prepare the food and serve the men first. Each family provided a dish.

Pennsylvania *Dietsch* echoed throughout the room as Kathryn made her way around, refilling cups and nodding to friends and family. Her eyes moved to a small table in the back of the room, off on its own away from the crowd, where an English couple, friends of her sister Beth Anne, sat chatting.

That's where Anna Mae and Kellan would sit—by themselves, away from the family.

The thought came to Kathryn before she could stop it. Her thoughts had been with Anna Mae during the service. Instead of concentrating on the bishop and ministers who had been preaching the Word, Kathryn found herself glancing over toward the English couple sitting in the back, off by themselves, during the service.

If Anna Mae and Kellan were to visit and attend a service, they too would sit alone, away from the family, like strangers —perhaps not strangers, but more like visitors instead of members of the family.

Finding her pitcher empty, Kathryn stepped back into the kitchen where Anna Mae's three sisters, Barbie, Vera, and Fannie, were flittering around the kitchen, preparing to bring out the cakes and cookies for dessert. Kathryn wondered how they would react to seeing their youngest sister again. Would they welcome her with open arms despite the pain of her leaving? Or would they be standoffish, giving her a mere nod and cold greeting when she arrived?

"Kathryn," Vera said, holding out a plate of cookies. "Would you take these out?"

"Of course," Kathryn said, taking the dish. She paused. "Have you heard from Anna Mae lately?"

Vera stopped and her eyes widened with surprise. "No, I haven't heard from her since last Christmas. She always sends me a card. Have you?"

Kathryn nodded. "I have."

"You have?" Vera asked. She turned to her sisters. "Fannie! Barbie! Kathryn's heard from Anna Mae."

The three sisters surrounded Kathryn.

Vera asked, "How is Anna Mae?"

"When did you hear from her?" Fannie demanded.

"Is she happy with that English man?" Barbie chimed in.

"She's doing well," Kathryn said, gripping the plate. "She and Kellan are very happy and are expecting their first baby."

The three sisters gasped and then fired off more questions about Anna Mae's life. Kathryn held up her hand, and they stopped speaking.

"The baby is due in January," Kathryn said. "Anna Mae and Kellan are both doing well. She said she misses the family and would like to reconnect with everyone for the sake of the baby." Kathryn bit her bottom lip, debating how much to share. "She wants to come visit."

"Oh." Barbie frowned. "I don't know how *Daed* would react to that."

Fannie nodded. "Probably not a good idea."

"I think it would be *wunderbaar gut*," Vera said. "When does she want to come?"

"She's still working out the details," Kathryn said.

"She should wait until after the baby is born," Fannie said while Barbie nodded in agreement. "That would help smooth things over with *Daed*."

"*Ya*," Barbie added.

"I disagree," Vera said, touching Kathryn's arm. "Any time would be *gut*. Her visit might be awkward, but it would start to mend some fences."

Kathryn glanced down at the cookies. "I better get these out to the men before they start complaining." She stepped out into the family room with Vera in tow.

"Does Anna Mae want to come soon?" Vera whispered.

Kathryn nodded. "*Ya*. Very soon."

Vera raised her eyebrows in question. "How soon?"

"For Christmas," Kathryn said.

Vera patted her arm. "Tell her to come. *Daed* and my siblings may be against her visit, but it would heal my *mamm's* broken heart."

Kathryn smiled. "I'll do that."

Later that evening, Kathryn waited until David was snoring before she padded downstairs to the kitchen and found her stationery in the drawer. In the light of the gas lantern, she wrote a letter to Anna Mae, outlining the plans for her trip. After signing it, she sealed it in the envelope and addressed it. She then placed it in the pocket of her apron hanging on the peg in the kitchen and tiptoed up to bed.

As she snuggled down under the covers next to David, Kathryn whispered a prayer to God, telling Him that she hoped she was honoring His wishes and asking Him to use her as He saw fit to bring the Beiler family back together for Christmas.

CHAPTER 5

Anna Mae clutched the letter and sank into the kitchen chair. Tears filled her eyes as she studied the words written in Kathryn's beautiful cursive writing.

Dear Anna Mae,

I hope this letter finds you and Kellan well. Please know you're in my daily prayers.

As I'm writing to you, my heart is filled with excitement. After we talked last week I prayed and asked God to show me a sign that I was doing His will by helping you plan a trip here for Christmas. The next day I received the message from God that I'd been hoping for when your mamm came to visit me at the bakery.

Anna Mae, your mamm shared with me that you've been on her mind and in her heart for some time now. She said she thinks of you constantly, wondering if you're gut and froh with your life in Baltimore. She shared with me that she would love to see you, and I know that's what God would want.

Today I attended church at your sister Vera's home, and I spoke to her about your possible visit. Vera was

*excited and told me that having you visit would be a
wunderbaar way to help bring the family back together.
She said that while the visit may be strained at first,
having you here would begin to mend fences.*

*I've arranged for you and Kellan to stay at the
Paradise Inn Bed and Breakfast from December 22–24,
checking out on Christmas morning. You are welcome
to have dinner with us that first night, and from there
we will make arrangements to see the rest of the family.
Please let me know if that will be convenient for you.*

*I'm keeping your visit a secret. Only my mamm
Amanda, and Vera know that you're planning to come,
and we'll keep it to ourselves until you get here. As I said
above, I know that your initial arrival may be awkward,
but I'll be by your side to help work through that. Once
your parents see you and find out that you're expecting
a baby, they will be willing to work things out in order to
have you, Kellan, and the baby in their life.*

I can't wait to hug you and talk to you in person.

In His Name,
Kathryn

She reread the letter and sniffed, tears flowing from her
eyes.

"Annie?" Kellan crossed the kitchen and crouched beside
her chair. "Honey, what's wrong?" He wiped tears from her
hot cheeks with the tip of his finger.

"*Mamm* misses me," she whispered, holding out the letter
to him. "She misses me like I miss her. And my sister Vera
wants to see me too. I miss my sisters so much."

While he read the letter, Anna Mae rubbed her abdomen and lost herself in memories of her family—the delicious smell of freshly baked bread in her mother's kitchen, the roar of her brother and cousins roughhousing in the yard, the *clip-clop* of horses coming up the lane with buggies packed with visitors. She wanted her child to experience all of that—all she loved and missed about being Amish.

Kellan met her gaze and kissed her cheek. "I'm so happy for you. I hope this visit gives you the peace and love you need from your family. If God sent Kathryn a sign, He is also sending us a sign that we need to go."

"Thank you! I'm so glad you agree!" She wrapped her arms around his neck, and he shifted his weight and chuckled.

"You're going to sweep me off my feet again, Annie." He took her hands in his and smiled. "You nearly knocked me over."

"I'm going to write her back tonight and tell her that we'll be there on the twenty-second." She hoisted herself from the chair and crossed the kitchen. "I only have a couple weeks until we go. I have so much to do." She fished a notepad and pen from a drawer and began a list. "We'll have to bring gifts for all of the children. I'm not quite sure what, though." She jotted down ideas for gifts, including candies and small toys.

"Gifts for all of the kids?" Kellan stood behind her. "How can we buy for all your relatives, Annie? Aren't there hundreds of kids now?"

Glancing up, she laughed. "I don't expect hundreds, but, yes, there are many children in the Beiler family. And I'll bring them little gifts, like candy and small toys. Don't worry; I won't break our budget. I'll visit the Dollar Mart in town after my quilting circle meeting." She jotted a few more things down on the list and then looked up. "Maybe we can run to the store tonight after supper. I think they're open late, and I'll need your help with the bags."

A smile spread across his lips. "I have an idea. How about we go to our favorite steak place and then go shopping?"

"Steak and shrimp?" She glanced down at her abdomen. "How does that sound, Butterbean?"

"Butterbean?" Kellan raised an eyebrow.

"I thought it was a cuter name than Lug Nut. I think Lug Nut sounds like a boy, and Butterbean could be a boy or a girl." She rubbed her belly. "Let me get my purse and we can head out." She kissed his cheek on her way to the hall.

Her heart skipped a beat as she thought of seeing her family again. She couldn't wait to hug her mother, Kathryn, and her sisters. And she hoped her father would be happy to see her too.

Thursday evening, Kathryn slipped the letter into her apron pocket and pulled plates from the cabinet in preparation for supper. A smile turned up the corners of her lips as she placed a bag of rolls onto the table. In less than two weeks, she would see her sister-in-law for the first time in three years, and her visit would bring the Beiler family together once again. The plan would come together solely due to Kathryn's efforts. If she were a proud person, Kathryn would gloat.

The letter outlined Anna Mae's plans. She and Kellan would check in at the Paradise B&B the afternoon of Wednesday, December 22, and have dinner with Kathryn and her family that night. Depending on how they were received, they would stay till Christmas, visiting and reconnecting with family and friends.

Kathryn's smile deepened. Mary Rose, Vera, and some of the other relatives would be ecstatic when they saw Anna Mae, and they would have Kathryn to thank for it.

But how would David feel about her going against his wishes? Would he feel betrayed? Her smile transformed to a frown, for she knew the answer to those questions. David hadn't mentioned Anna Mae since their last strained conversation. He would certainly be angry when Anna Mae arrived at their home, but she believed in her heart that he would forgive her soon after seeing his sister.

The back door squeaked open, revealing David entering the kitchen. He crossed the room to the sink and washed his hands. "The *kinner* are on their way in from the barn."

"I bet they're hungry," she said, placing a block of cheese on the table. She then grabbed a pot of soup from the stove. "I made some chicken noodle soup. It's cold out there, *ya*?"

"*Ya*," he said, drying his hands. "It's hard to believe *Grischtdaag* is only a few weeks away. The boys were just discussing what gifts they hope to find on the table Christmas morning. It feels like only yesterday it was summer. Where did the year go?"

"I don't know." Kathryn grabbed a stack of bowls. "It seems like the years pass by quicker, the older we get." She yanked open the drawer and reached for a handful of spoons and then placed the bowls and utensils on the table.

He snickered. "*Ya*. Some days I feel eighty instead of almost forty." Stopping her on her way back to the table, he pulled her into his arms and brushed his lips across hers, sending her stomach into a wild swirl. "But then you make me feel young again."

Kathryn wrapped her arms around his neck and inhaled his scent, earth mixed with soap. *"Ich liebe dich,* David." *And please forgive me for planning your sister's visit behind your back.*

He took her face in his hands and his eyes were full of love. "Katie, I thank God for you and our *kinner* every day. This year I'm most thankful for you and our life together."

She swallowed as the guilt of her secrecy rained down on her, then forced a smile. *"Danki.* I thank God for you daily too." *And I hope you'll still trust me after Anna Mae's visit.*

His eyes studied hers. "You all right?"

"Ya." She turned toward the counter. "I was just thinking about everything I need to do before *Grischtdaag.* I must get to the market. I'll need to see if Nina Janitz can take me shopping." She rooted around in a drawer in search of a notepad and a pencil. "I have to make a list."

"Katie." David took her hands in his. "Look at me."

She met his gaze, her heart pounding with a mixture of guilt and anxiety. *"Ya?"*

He traced her face, from forehead to chin, with his fingertip. *"Was iss letz, mei liewe?"*

"Nothing's wrong," she said, her voice quavering.

His brown eyes continued to probe hers, and her mouth dried. How was it that he could read her so well? She searched for something to say to change the subject.

"I wonder what's taking the *kinner* so long," she said. "Should you go check on them? Amanda and Lizzie are up-

stairs working on a sewing project. I'll go call them again."
She started for the stairs, and he took her arm and pulled
her back.

"Wait," he said, looking concerned. "If something is bothering you, you can tell me. There should be no secrets between a man and his *fraa*."

She sighed. She had to tell him the truth, and now was
the appropriate time. "David, I just wish you would recon-
sider your thoughts on Anna Mae's visit."

His concerned look transformed to a grimace. "I told you
that this subject was closed. We'll go visit her in the spring.
Now, please drop it."

She scowled. "Why can't we discuss it? Why must you tell
me when the subject is closed without my input?"

He raised his hand to his temple, pinching his forehead.
"I'm tired of having this argument, Kathryn."

She jammed her hands on her hips. "I am too. I want you
to listen to me. I think it's a *gut* idea. Christmas is the best
time for a family reunion. Why can't you even consider it?"

He gritted his teeth. "Because I know how painful it will
be for my parents, and I don't want to ruin Christmas for
them. It would be more appropriate if we waited until spring
to visit Anna Mae and Kellan. Once we visit with them, then
we can pave the way for my parents to see them. I know
what's best for my family, Kathryn."

"You do?"

"*Mamm? Daed?*" a little voice asked. "Why are you
fighting?"

Kathryn turned to find Lizzie standing in the doorway,
her brown eyes wide with fear. Amanda moved up behind

her and placed her hand on Lizzie's shoulder, and Kathryn's heart sank. She'd managed to scare her daughter by arguing with David.

"Everything's fine," Kathryn said. "Dinner is ready."

The back door opened and slammed with a bang, and David Jr., Manny, and Ruthie marched into the kitchen, chattering away about Christmas and what toys they hoped to receive while hanging their wraps and coats on the pegs.

"Wash up, please," Kathryn said, feeling David's eyes boring into her. Ignoring his stare, she brought a pitcher of water to the table. "Did you and Lizzie finish that dress you were working on?" she asked Amanda.

"We're almost done," Amanda said, placing cups at each table setting while Lizzie distributed the plates and bowls. "Lizzie is doing a *wunderbaar* job. She'll be making her own dresses soon."

David glared up at Kathryn while she poured water into his cup and she averted her eyes by concentrating on not spilling. Once the table was set, Kathryn sat between Amanda and Lizzie while the rest of the children took their spot at the table. David gave her one last hard look before bowing his head in silent prayer. A chill of worry coursed through her.

Kathryn bowed her head. She thanked God for the wonderful blessings of her family and home and then she asked Him to guide Anna Mae's visit. She prayed the Lord would open her father-in-law's heart so he would welcome Anna Mae and Kellan home to Lancaster County.

But most of all, she prayed that David would forgive her and understand why she defied his wishes and helped plan Anna Mae's trip.

CHAPTER 6

The days before Christmas flew by in a blur of shopping, baking, and chores, so Kathryn rarely had a spare moment to think about Anna Mae's visit. The week of Christmas finally arrived, and Kathryn rushed around the kitchen Monday evening preparing supper. While a ham loaf baked in the oven, she placed a pot of mixed vegetables on the stove and then turned to Amanda, who was busy peeling potatoes. "Are the boys outside doing their chores?"

"*Ya*. Lizzie and Ruthie are upstairs cleaning our room," Amanda said, her pretty face scowling. "*Mamm*, I wanted to speak with you about something in private."

Kathryn raised her eyebrows with curiosity while wiping her hands on a towel. "What's on your mind?"

Amanda glanced across the kitchen. "I don't want anyone to hear us."

"You just said that the boys were outside and your sisters are upstairs, so I'm certain we're alone." Kathryn leaned against the counter. "*Was iss letz?*"

Amanda glanced back toward the door. "Let's go into the *schtupp*."

Kathryn followed her into the family room and stood near the doorway. "What's bothering you?"

Amanda lowered her slight body onto the sofa.

"I'm worried about what's going to happen this week." Amanda wrung her hands. "*Daed* might get really angry that *Aenti* Anna Mae is coming."

Kathryn smiled. "Everything will be fine once he sees his sister. Trust me." A door closed, and Kathryn assumed the boys had come in from the barn.

"But he should know the truth." Amanda's eyes were full of determination.

"*Ya*, you're right." Kathryn nodded. "He'll know the truth soon enough. It's going to be a surprise."

"I think you're wrong not to tell him. I feel like I'm holding in a horrible lie by not telling *Daed*, and lying is a sin." Amanda shook her head. "I think *Daed* has a right to know that *Aenti* Anna Mae is coming—" She stopped speaking and her eyes grew wide while her cheeks flushed a deep rose.

"What did you say, Amanda Joy?" David's gruff voice rumbled from behind Kathryn, causing her to jump.

Kathryn spun around and her mouth dried. David was glowering at her from the doorway.

"What did Amanda say about *mei schweschder?*" he asked, his brown eyes slicing through her with indignation.

Kathryn inwardly shuddered. Feigning indifference, she kept her expression serene. "She was discussing when our company would arrive," she said, standing up straighter and mustering all of the courage she could find inside herself. "Amanda was telling me that she thinks you have a right to know that Anna Mae and Kellan are going to join us for

Christmas this year." The truth was now out in the open. She felt a mixture of relief and anxiety at the opportunity to finally say the words out loud.

David's expression hardened. "Kathryn, how many times do we have to discuss this?" His voice was low and full of frustration and fury. "I've already told you that I am against this visit. I can't think of how I could make it more clear to you."

"You've made yourself perfectly clear. However, the plans have been made." She looked at Amanda, who was studying her hands in her lap. "Amanda, our company will arrive sometime Wednesday afternoon."

Amanda met her gaze with a worried expression, and Kathryn smiled, hoping to calm her. Ruthie and Lizzie entered the family room with wide smiles on their faces.

"Company?" Ruthie asked.

"Who's coming?" Lizzie chimed in.

"Your *Aenti* Anna Mae and *Onkel* Kellan from Baltimore are coming to spend Christmas with us," Kathryn said, ignoring the feel of David's angry stare boring into her. "*Aenti* Anna Mae is your *dat's* youngest *schweschder.*"

"The one who was shunned?" Ruthie asked.

"*Ya.*" Kathryn nodded. "That's right."

"Are they staying here?" Lizzie asked while sinking down onto the sofa next to Amanda.

"They can sleep in my bed with me," Ruthie said, walking over to Kathryn.

Kathryn smiled. "That's very thoughtful, Ruthie, but they're staying at a bed and breakfast in Paradise."

"But we'll see them, *ya*?" Ruthie asked.

"*Ya*, we will see them," Kathryn said. She pushed a lock of hair back from where it had fallen from beneath her prayer *kapp* while avoiding David's eyes. "They'll be visiting for a few days."

"Kathryn," David said, his calmness forced. "Kathryn, please look at me."

"*Ya*." She turned to him, finding disappointment and hurt reflecting in his eyes. Guilt and determination battled inside her. While she knew keeping the information from him was wrong, she was certain she was doing God's will. God was using her to heal the family, and David needed to understand that.

His frown deepened. "We will discuss this later at length."

Kathryn nodded while forcing a smile. "I'm certain we will."

"Call me when supper is ready," David said, stomping through the family room toward the stairs.

Kathryn glanced at Lizzie. "Would you and Ruthie please set the table?" While her two younger daughters headed for the kitchen, she turned to Amanda. "Now he knows."

Amanda nodded, her cheeks still glowing red. "He was very angry. I made it worse, didn't I?"

Kathryn shook her head. "No, you didn't make it worse, but this wasn't the way I wanted him to find out."

Amanda's lower lip quivered, and her eyes filled with tears. "I'm sorry, *Mamm*."

Kathryn touched Amanda's arm. "You didn't do anything wrong. You were right to talk to me about it if it bothered you."

"I didn't know he was standing there until it was too late,"

Amanda said with a sniff. "He must've come in quietly and heard us talking."

"I'm certain he did." Kathryn gestured toward the door. "Come help me make the dumplings. The ham loaf smells like it's almost done."

Amanda stood and walked with her toward the kitchen. Kathryn was certain that David would be quiet during supper and leave the discussion of Anna Mae's visit for bedtime. Dread filled Kathryn at the thought of facing him. She hoped David would understand why she'd gone against his wishes.

Kathryn ran a brush through her waist-length hair and studied her reflection. Clad in her nightgown, she glanced toward the door for the fourth time. The clock on the wall told her it was nearly nine, David's daily bedtime.

He'd barely spoken to her during supper and had only given terse answers to her lame attempts at fostering a conversation. Instead of conversing with her, he'd spoken to the children about their day. After supper, David had disappeared outside with Junior, which they often did in the evenings. However, she'd heard Junior come back into the house and disappear into his room awhile ago, but she'd not seen David.

Stepping over to the window, she moved the dark green shade and peeked outside. The barn and backfield were dark with no sign of a lantern.

The bedroom door squeaked open and banged shut, and Kathryn jumped with a start.

"Sorry," David mumbled, scowling. "I didn't mean to

slam it." He stepped over to his bureau and pulled off his suspenders.

Her heart pounded as she sat on the edge of the bed. "Where were you?"

"In the barn," he muttered, shucking off his shirt.

She pushed an errant lock of golden blonde hair behind her shoulder. "What were you doing in the barn?"

"Thinking." He changed into his pajama pants. "Actually, trying to figure something out."

The tension between them was suffocating her. She had to apologize to him and make things right. She took a deep breath. "David, I—"

"Would you like to know what I was trying to figure out?"

"David, please—"

He stood before her and held a hand up to keep her from talking. "Let me finish."

Knowing she wasn't going to earn a chance to speak her mind, Kathryn crossed her arms in front of her chest. "Go on."

"I was trying to figure out why you would go behind my back and do something I'd asked you not to do, especially after we'd discussed it several times." Still glowering, he pulled up a chair and sat before her. "I'd asked you not to invite Anna Mae. I told you, no I *promised* you, that we would visit her this spring. I also said that once we visited her and Kellan, we would make plans for her to come back to the community to visit the family. From what I remember, you said that would be a *gut* plan."

Kathryn opened her mouth to defend herself, and he again held up his hand to stop her.

"Please let me finish." He sat up straight. "What I've been trying to figure out is why you went against my wishes. What makes it even worse is that you not only broke a promise and went behind my back, but you involved our *kinner* in your lies." He shook his head, disappointment clouding his handsome face. "What hurts the most is that you lied. In our fifteen years of marriage, I never once lied to you or went behind your back. You've always been the one person I've trusted most, the one I knew I could count on."

Shaking his head, he paused. "Now, I'm trying to figure out who you are. The *maedel* I married would have never lied to me, not like this. You knew how serious I was about this and how much I was against inviting Anna Mae home during the holidays. This is going to cause a huge blowup with my *daed*, and I'm not prepared to deal with that."

The knot forming in her throat choked off her words for a moment. She cleared her throat before she tried to speak again. "David, I've never lied to you before," she began, her voice trembling with guilt. "You're the most important person in my life, aside from our *kinner*. You know that and you know me." She pointed to her chest. "You know my heart."

"But we talked about it over and over again. I told you more than once that it was not a *gut* plan. We decided that we would wait until spring. Why did you go back on your word?"

"I never agreed to spring." She reached for him, and he stood, backing away from her touch. "David, will you let me explain?"

Folding his arms, he leaned back against the wall and scowled. "I'm listening."

She stood in front of him. "I know in my heart that what I'm doing is right. It's God's will that Anna Mae and Kellan are coming here." She took his hand in hers. "God spoke to me."

He raised an eyebrow with curiosity. "What do you mean?"

"I prayed about it and asked Him to give me a sign." Hot tears spilled from her eyes. "The very next day, your *mamm* came to the bakery and told me she's been thinking of Anna Mae and Kellan and wondering how they're doing. She was near tears and said she longed to see Anna Mae again. She said she had to know if Anna Mae was happy with her life with Kellan." She squeezed his hand. "That was the sign from God I needed. That was how I knew what I was doing was right."

He considered her words and his frown deepened. "A sign from God?" He snorted with disbelief. "I don't know about that, Kathryn. God has a plan, and it's His plan. He doesn't need to send us signs."

"*Ya*, He does! You have to believe me. I never meant to hurt you and I don't want to ever lose your trust in me." More tears splattered her cheeks. "Can't you see that? Can't you see I did this for you and our family? This is what God wants me to do."

"I don't believe God has to send us signs for us to do His work. His rules for how we should live our lives are contained in the Bible. Whether you believe He sent a sign or not doesn't matter. You deliberately went against my wishes, and I'm angry and hurt." His expression remained hard as stone. "Why did you keep your secret from me?"

"I followed my heart because I didn't want you to talk me out of it. I wanted to do it, no matter what you said." She cleared her throat. "I wanted to do it for Mary Rose. I can't imagine how I would feel if one of our *kinner* had moved away and left the community. I would worry about her too. Your *mamm* has a right to meet her future grandchild."

He shook his head. "That's not for you to decide. Now Christmas is going to be a disaster."

"That's not true." Kathryn wiped her tears. "Vera agrees that this visit is a good idea too. She thinks it'll be good for your parents."

His eyes widened. "You told Vera?" He frowned. "Who else have you told?"

"My mother knows too," she whispered.

He threw his hands up. "Why don't you just paint a sign on the side of the barn so that the whole district knows!"

"David," she hissed. "You're going to wake the *kinner*!"

"Why not tell them too?" he continued, his voice booming off the walls. "The rest of the district already knows." He started toward the door. "I'll go tell my father now."

"David!" Kathryn rushed after him and pulled him back. "Now you're acting *narrisch*!"

"I'm *narrisch*?" He snorted with sarcasm. "I'm not seeing signs from God involving everyone but my spouse in secret plans." He shook his head. "I especially don't like that you involved Amanda. I don't want you to teach our *dochdern* to defy their future husbands."

Kathryn shook her head. He didn't comprehend her motive, and she couldn't think of anything else to say to try to get through to him. "You don't understand why I did this at all, do you?"

"No, I don't." He folded his arms across his wide chest. "What will this visit entail? I know she's arriving Wednesday and staying in Paradise. What else have you planned without my knowledge?"

"We're hosting them for supper Wednesday. Thursday night we'll also invite your parents."

He raised an eyebrow. "I'm sure your mother supports all of this."

"She also believes it's God's will for our family to heal." She reached for his arm, but he stepped away from her touch. "I truly believe that, David. That's why I did it. My best intentions were for our family. I didn't want to cause you to be upset with me."

"You know my *daed*." He frowned. "He won't be as *eiferich* as the rest of the Beilers."

"We can all pray for his heart to be opened and warmed by the sight of his youngest *dochder* and his future grandchild."

"This is going to be a huge mistake." He shook his head and started for the door.

"Where are you going?" she asked.

"Downstairs to read my Bible and think," he said.

"But it's after nine," she said.

"I'm not ready to sleep. You go ahead to bed," he said.

She watched him disappear into the hallway and close the door behind him. Sighing, she climbed into bed. For the first time in their sixteen years of marriage, she was going to bed alone. Ironically, Kathryn's plans for bringing the family together had seemed to tear David and her apart. Tears filled her eyes at the thought of the chasm she'd put between herself and her husband.

Shivering, she pulled the quilt up to her chin and closed her eyes, hoping somehow Christmas would turn out better than David expected.

CHAPTER 7

Anna Mae's stomach fluttered as their burgundy Chevrolet Equinox took another winding hill. She gripped the door handle as more snow flurries peppered the windshield.

"You okay?" Kellan reached over and covered her hand with his warm palm.

"Don't you think you should slow down?" she asked. "The snow is picking up."

"We're fine," he said with a confident smile. "I know how to drive in snow. You forget I went to college in Maine. This is nothing compared to the blizzards I saw up there."

"I hear it's going to snow most of the week and may be pretty bad on Christmas." Anna Mae turned to him. "Now, you remember that Amish Christmases are different from English Christmases. They don't put up a tree or include Santa. They may do a little bit of decorating with poinsettias and candles, but you won't see any Christmas lights. To the Amish, it's more about family and Jesus' birth, not Santa and gifts."

Kellan nodded. "I remember that. You've explained it to me before."

"And they have First Christmas and Second Christmas,"

she reminisced. "In our family, we received our gifts on Christmas morning. My mother set up the table especially for the kids, and it was called the Christmas table. She put our names by each place setting and placed our gifts on the plate. We visited our extended family on Second Christmas, which was the twenty-sixth, and shared a huge meal. It was so much fun playing with all of our cousins. My grandparents would give each of us a little gift, like candy."

"Sounds like a lot of visiting," Kellan commented.

Kathryn laughed. "Since Amish families are so large, they have lots of get-togethers. Some have their Christmas dinners as early as Thanksgiving." She shifted in the seat and a sharp pain radiated through her abdomen, causing her to suck in a breath.

"Are you all right?" Kellan's voice was full of alarm.

Anna Mae took short, quick breaths until the discomfort subsided. "I'm fine. Thank you." She heaved a sigh of relief. "It's gone now. No worries." She smiled, in spite of his distressed expression.

"I was concerned about your traveling this close to the due date," he said, his eyes trained on the road. "The doctor said the risk of preterm labor or complications goes up after week thirty."

Anna Mae rubbed her abdomen. "Yes, but she gave us permission to go on this trip since we're within ninety miles of her office. We're only about eighty miles from home, so if something should happen, we can get back to the hospital quickly. I'm sure we'll be fine."

He negotiated another sharp turn. "Promise me that you'll tell me if you start feeling different or if the pain becomes more frequent. I'll get you to Lancaster General in the blink of an eye."

She settled back in the seat. "I'm sure that won't be necessary, but I promise I will. I think Butterbean has several weeks before she decides to make her entrance into the world."

The SUV rounded another corner and a brick colonial home came into view. A large sign with the words "Paradise Bed & Breakfast" stood by the sweeping enclosed porch facing the road. A cobblestone pathway led from the sidewalk to the front door. White Christmas lights outlined the home, and a tree decorated with silver and blue ornaments and white lights sat by a large window in the enclosed porch.

Kellan steered into the gravel parking area next to the house and nosed the SUV up to the wall. "Here we are," he said. "It was nice of them to agree to an early check-in. We'll get rid of our luggage and then we can do whatever you'd like. This is your trip, Annie."

He climbed from the truck and then came around to her side of the vehicle. Opening her door, he offered his hand.

"I'm fine," she said, struggling to hoist herself from the seat.

"Are you?" He laughed and took her hand. Lifting her up, he smirked. "Now you're fine."

She gave him a mock glare. "I could've done it myself."

"And how long would that have taken you? I don't have that kind of time. The reservation is only for three nights." His grin was wicked.

"Ha, ha," she muttered. Glancing down, she spotted her purse on the floorboard of the SUV and swallowed a groan.

"I'll get it." He handed her the purse, then kissed her cheek. "Go on inside. I'll get the bags."

Anna Mae schlepped up the cobblestone path, silently wishing she'd worn her boots instead of these stupid, uncomfortable loafers that had become too tight in the last week. It seemed everything was too tight, even her maternity clothes. She quickly changed her mind about her due date and hoped Butterbean would make his or her appearance soon. However, she did hope it wasn't *too* soon.

The tiny flakes of snow kissed her warm cheeks, and she inhaled the moist air. It smelled like home. She smiled to herself. Three years had been too long to stay away.

Kellan weaved past her with a bag over his shoulder and a suitcase trailing behind him, the wheels scraping the cobblestones. He held the door open, and Anna Mae stepped into a hallway lined with a steep staircase, loveseat, and bookshelves. Kellan directed Anna Mae to the loveseat and set the luggage down next to her before stepping into the kitchen and greeting the bed and breakfast owners.

The older couple led Kellan and Anna Mae to a large bedroom located off the hallway, and Anna Mae was thankful to not have to climb the long staircase.

While Anna Mae freshened up, Kellan brought in the rest of their luggage. Once they were settled in the room, Kellan took Anna Mae's hand and led her back to the SUV, where he helped her climb in.

Kellan hopped into the driver's seat and fastened his safety belt. "So, where are we going?" he asked, turning the key and bringing the engine back to life with a purr.

"Let's head toward Bird-in-Hand," she said, her heart thumping at the thought.

He grinned. "To the site where I first laid eyes on your beautiful face?"

She nodded.

"I still remember the way." He put the SUV in reverse and backed out of the parking space. He then steered it toward the main road.

They rode in silence with the only sound coming from the quiet hum of the engine, the occasional whisper of windshield wipers clearing away the flurries, and the Christmas music singing softly through the speakers.

Anna Mae stared out the window while memories danced through her mind. Excitement and anxiety coursed through her while they drove.

As they turned onto Gibbons Road, her heart raced. Soon she would see her sister-in-law for the first time in three years. Would their reunion be as wonderful as she'd dreamed? What if Anna Mae felt awkward and out of place? What if they had nothing to discuss and they merely stood in silence, studying each other and thinking of how different they had become?

She said a silent prayer that her family would welcome her and be happy to see her.

Kellan's warm hand covered hers. "It'll be fine, Annie. They'll be so happy to see you that they'll all cry. You'll see."

She squeezed his hand. "You always seem to read my mind."

He lifted her hand to his lips and kissed it. "That's my job, dear." He nodded toward the windshield. "Here we are."

Anna Mae's stomach flip-flopped as they pulled into the parking lot of the bakery. It looked just as she remembered. The large white clapboard farmhouse sat near the road and included a sweeping wraparound porch. A sign with "Kauffman Amish Bakery" in old-fashioned letters hung above the door.

Out behind the building was a fenced-in play area where in the warmer months the Kauffman grandchildren would run around, play tag, and climb on a huge wooden swing set. Beyond it was a fenced pasture dotted with patches of snow. A few of the large Kauffman family farmhouses and barns were set back beyond the pasture. The dirt road leading to the other homes was roped off with a sign declaring "Private Property—No Trespassing."

A large paved parking lot sat adjacent to the building. Kellan steered the SUV into a parking space near the entrance of the bakery and put the truck in park. He then pulled the keys from the ignition and faced Anna Mae.

"Ready?" he asked.

Anna Mae sucked in a deep breath, her heart pounding against her ribcage. "I guess I'm as ready as I'll ever be." She gripped the door handle.

"Hey." Kellan touched her shoulder, and she faced him. "Don't forget what I told you before we came here. No matter what happens with your family, I'll always love you. What matters is that we have each other." He touched her belly. "We're a family whether your father accepts you back or not."

She touched his face. "Thank you for bringing me here. I couldn't do it without you."

He kissed her hand. "You're stronger than you think,

Annie." He squeezed her hand. "Let's go in. I'm sure the Kauffmans are anxious to see you."

Anna Mae grasped Kellan's hand as they made their way through the swirling snow flurries to the front door of the bakery.

Her pulse quickened when he opened the door, and the little bell chimed, announcing their arrival. She breathed in the delicious scents of freshly baked bread and chocolate. She glanced around the bakery, which looked just as it had three years ago, with the long counter filled with pastries and the array of shelves and displays packed with Amish Country souvenirs. A half-dozen small tables, each with four chairs, sat by the window, welcoming tourists to sit and enjoy their pastries.

She spotted Kathryn, Elizabeth, and a pretty teenager who resembled Kathryn standing by the counter.

"Anna Mae!" Kathryn cried, meeting her gaze. Kathryn looked exactly as Anna Mae recalled. She had the same golden blonde hair pulled tight in a bun under her prayer covering. Her eyes were still a deep shade of powder blue, and her skin was as clear and porcelain as a doll. She rushed across the bakery with her mother and the girl in tow and engulfed Anna Mae in her arms.

Anna Mae held onto her sister-in-law as tears spilled from her eyes. She inhaled Kathryn's scent—lilac mixed with cinnamon—and smiled.

Stepping back from the hug, Kathryn studied Anna Mae. "Let me look at you. You're still *schee*." She gestured to Anna Mae's stomach. "You look *wunderbaar*!" She turned to Elizabeth. "*Mamm*, doesn't she look lovely?"

The three women began prattling away in Pennsylvania *Dietsch*, and Anna Mae looked between them, trying to resurrect her fluency. The words clicked through her mind, and she suddenly felt as if she'd never left. Her first language fit like her favorite winter gloves. She answered in *Dietsch* their questions about how her trip had gone.

Anna Mae looked at the girl. "Amanda," she said. "You're so *schee*. You look just like your *mamm*!"

"*Danki*," Amanda said.

Anna Mae took Kellan's hand and pulled him to her side. "You'll have to speak English for Kellan. We don't speak *Dietsch* at home."

Kathryn and Elizabeth exchanged smiles.

Anna Mae nodded toward them. "Kellan, you remember Kathryn, Elizabeth, and Amanda, right?"

He shook their hands. "It's so good to see you again. You all look well."

Elizabeth smiled. "I can tell you're taking good care of Anna Mae. Thank you."

Anna Mae hugged Elizabeth and then Amanda.

"You're all grown up," Anna Mae said to Amanda. "I bet you don't even remember me."

"Of course I remember you, *Aenti* Anna Mae," her niece said. "You're the *aenti* who used to play dolls with me when I stayed at *grossmammi's* house."

"That's right." Anna Mae touched her shoulder. "I'm glad you remember that."

"Let's all sit down and visit." Elizabeth pointed toward a table with chairs on the other side of the bakery. "Amanda and I will grab some drinks and snacks."

Looping her arm around Anna Mae's shoulders, Kathryn steered her toward the table. "Does the bakery look the same to you?"

"Oh yes," Anna Mae said, scanning the shelves of pastries and mementos. "I feel as if I never left."

"Do you miss it?" Kellan asked.

Anna Mae shrugged. "It's hard to say. I do, but I don't. I don't regret leaving, but I do miss my family." She smiled up at Kathryn, who squeezed her shoulder.

"We miss you too." She gestured toward the chairs. "Please sit. I want to hear all about the *boppli*. Do you know if you're having a boy or a girl?"

Anna Mae shook her head. "No, we decided we want to be surprised. Kellan is sure we're having a boy, but I think there's a possibility it may be a girl."

"When are you due?" Kathryn asked.

"January fifteen," Anna Mae said, sinking into the chair. "But some days it feels sooner."

"Oh?" Kathryn raised her eyebrows. "Was it smart for you to travel so close to your due date?"

"See?" Kellan tapped the table. "I'm not the only one who is concerned about you, Annie."

Anna Mae frowned at Kathryn. "Don't encourage him. He worries too much."

"That's my job." Kellan slipped off his coat. "Do you need help taking off your wrap?"

"No, I'm fine, thank you." Anna Mae pulled off her cloak. "To answer your question, the doctor gave me permission to travel. I shouldn't have any problems, and we're only about eighty miles from home. If something were to happen, we can get back to the hospital quickly." She glanced at Kathryn, who was smiling. "What is it?"

"You're glowing, Anna Mae." Reaching over, Kathryn squeezed her hand. "You look so *wunderbaar,* so *froh.* Your *mamm* is going to be thrilled. Tell me all about your life in Baltimore."

Anna Mae shared stories about the car dealership and her quilting ministry at church. Soon, Elizabeth and Amanda joined them with mugs of hot chocolate and cookies. Anna Mae enjoyed the warm cookies while Kathryn, Elizabeth, and Amanda filled Anna Mae and Kellan in on the latest community news.

When Anna Mae yawned, Kellan rubbed her shoulder. "I think you've had too much excitement. We should go back to the room, so you can rest before dinner." He nodded toward her belly. "He needs his rest too, you know."

Anna Mae shook her head. "You coddle me too much."

"Enjoy it now," Kathryn said with a laugh. "The focus will be on the baby once he's here."

"I'm sure that's how it will be." Anna Mae turned to Kellan. "A nap sounds like a wonderful idea. I am tired from the trip."

"I hope you can still join us for dinner," Kathryn said. "Tonight you can see our family before you visit with everyone else. David will be so anxious to see you, and the *kinner* are excited too."

"Do David and the *kinner* know we're here?" Anna Mae asked.

Amanda frowned. "He overheard my *mamm* and me talking about your visit Monday night. I didn't mean for him to hear, but at the same time, I felt like he needed to know."

"It's okay." Anna Mae smiled and then turned to Kathryn. "Is David okay with it? The visit, I mean."

Kathryn gave a slight shrug. "He was upset at first when he found out I'd planned it without his consent. He's concerned that your parents aren't going to take it well, but I believe that this visit is going to heal some family wounds." Reaching over, she touched Anna Mae's hand. "I think it will go just fine."

"Do my parents know we're here?" Anna Mae asked, praying that they were happy if they did know.

Kathryn shook her head. "No, but my family and Vera know. Before we try to see the rest of the family, we thought it best that you see how things go with *Daed* first."

"That's a good plan, but I would like to try to see my sisters too." Anna Mae turned to Kellan. "I guess we'll head back to the bed and breakfast for now."

"Sounds good." He looked at Kathryn. "What time should we be at your house for supper?"

"Five o'clock." Kathryn stood. "Does that sound *gut*?"

"Sounds fine. Can we bring anything?" he asked.

Kathryn waved off the question. "Don't be silly. We'll have plenty to eat. You just be sure Anna Mae takes a *gut* nap so she can enjoy our company."

"I'll get a good rest. Don't you worry about that." Anna took Kathryn's hands in hers. "Thank you for everything. It's so good to be here with you again. It's been too long."

"*Ya*, it has." Kathryn hugged her. "I look forward to seeing you in a few hours."

"Me too." Anna Mae took Kellan's hand and started for the door. "We'll see you later."

"You rest up now," Kathryn called. "I don't want you in the hospital while you're here."

"I will," Anna Mae promised. Stepping outside, she noticed that the snow flurries had picked up.

Kellan hooked his arm into hers as they headed for the truck. "You better tell me if you get too tired out. I don't want anything happening to you."

"I'll be fine." She rested her head on his shoulder. "Don't worry about me."

That evening Anna Mae and Kellan walked up the front path toward David and Kathryn's farmhouse. She grasped his hand and stopped him before they reached the door. "Let's wait a minute before we go in."

"You look beautiful." He brushed a lock of hair back from her face. "You have nothing to be nervous about, Annie. They're your family, and Kathryn invited you to come."

Smiling, she swiped a snowflake that had landed on his nose. "I'm sure visiting with my family won't be the most exciting way for you to spend your time off, but it means a lot to me. Thank you. Or maybe I should say *danki*."

"How do you say you're welcome?" he asked.

Anna Mae smiled. "*Gern gschehne.*"

He pulled her into his arms. "*Gern gschehne.*" He brushed his lips against hers, and courage surged through her.

"*Danki*," she said. "I needed that. Now let's go see my

brother and his family." Taking his hand in hers, Anna Mae climbed the porch steps and knocked on the door.

Voices sounded on the other side of the door before it opened, revealing four children, two boys and two girls, staring wide-eyed at Anna Mae and Kellan. All four were blonde like Kathryn. The girls were miniature versions of Amanda, and the boys reminded Anna Mae of her brother as a child.

"You're our English aunt!" a little girl said.

"*Aenti* Anna Mae," the other girl said.

Amanda marched toward them, frowning at her siblings. "Lizzie, Ruthie, Junior, and Manny," she snapped. "Please step back and let *Aenti* Anna Mae and *Onkel* Kellan come into the house." After the children backed away from the door, she turned to Anna Mae. "They're excited to see you. Please come in."

Kellan held the door and Anna Mae stepped in. The warmth from the fireplace seeped beneath her wrap while the aroma of roasted turkey and potatoes caused her stomach to growl.

The children swarmed around her, asking questions and rattling off their names. Tears filled Anna Mae's eyes as she spoke with them. It warmed her heart to be with her family again.

"Anna Mae," a voice bellowed above the chorus of children's voices.

Glancing up, Anna Mae found her brother David studying her, his brown eyes glistening. He looked just as she remembered: he was tall but stocky with his sandy blond hair cut in a traditional Amish bowl cut. His beard had grown longer during the past few years. Although a few lines around his eyes revealed he was closing in on forty, he still wore youthfulness in his face.

"David," she whispered, stepping over to him. "How are you?"

He nodded and gave a little smile. "I'm *gut*. How are you?"

Tears spilled from her eyes. "It's so good to see you."

"*Ya*," he said, his voice thick. "It's *gut* to see you too." He then looked at Kellan. "How are you?"

"I'm doing well." Kellan shook his hand. "How are you?"

"*Gut, gut.*" David gestured toward the family room. "Please come in." He glanced toward the children. "Go wash up. It's time to eat." He then looked back at Anna Mae. "Kathryn told me that you're expecting your baby soon. Congratulations."

"Thank you," Anna Mae said. "We're very excited." She took Kellan's hand in hers. "It's a dream come true. God has finally seen fit to make us parents."

David nodded. "That's *gut*. How are things in Baltimore?"

"Going well," Anna Mae said. "I work part-time in the office at Kellan's Chevrolet dealership, and I also run a quilting ministry at our church. Both keep me busy." She rubbed her abdomen in response to a kick. "Of course, I'll have to cut back after the baby is born." She touched David's arm. "How about you? Are you still working for *Daed* at the farm supply store?"

David absently pulled on his beard. "*Ya*, I am. We keep very busy."

"How are *Mamm* and *Daed*?" she asked.

"Doing *gut*." David shook his head. "*Daed* is the same. Still stubborn. *Mamm* is still a sweet angel and hasn't changed a bit."

"*Wie geht's?*" Kathryn came around the corner from the kitchen and hugged Anna Mae and shook Kellan's hand. "I hope you both brought your appetite." She gestured toward the table. "Everything is ready for you."

They sat at the table with the family, and Anna Mae silently marveled that Kathryn hadn't asked them to sit at a separate table alone since she was shunned. It warmed her heart that Kathryn and David included them as part of the family.

During dinner Anna Mae, Kathryn, and David reminisced about relatives and old friends. Anna Mae also listened to stories told by her nieces and nephews about their friends and school. They laughed so much that her abdomen and lower back were sore by the end of the meal.

After supper, they sat in the family room and ate cookies and talked about old times until nearly nine o'clock.

When Anna Mae began to yawn, Kellan stood and placed his hand on her shoulder. "I think you've had enough excitement for tonight," he said, rubbing her shoulder. "You should get some rest, and we'll visit again tomorrow."

Anna Mae covered his hand with hers. "You're probably right." She glanced over at Kathryn. "Everything was *wunderbaar.* Thank you so much for arranging this visit."

"Don't be silly," Kathryn said, waving off the comment. "It was no problem at all. We're just glad you're here." She took David's hand in hers and looked at him. "Right, David?"

"*Ya.*" He smiled at Anna Mae. "We're very happy you're here."

Anna Mae and Kellan stood and collected their coats.

They then hugged and kissed the children before heading for the door.

"You must join us for supper again tomorrow night," Kathryn said. "We'll have some guests along with you."

Anna Mae's heart leapt in her chest. "My parents?"

"*Ya.*" Kathryn nodded. "It will be fine. Have faith."

Anna Mae looked at her brother. "How do you think *Daed* will take my visit?"

"I pray it goes well." David's expression didn't mirror the certainty of his words.

"Same time tomorrow night?" Kathryn asked.

"That sounds perfect." Anna Mae hugged Kathryn and shook David's hand before she and Kellan headed to the SUV.

While they drove down the road, Anna Mae sniffed back tears. Overwhelmed by the emotion of seeing her brother and his family again, she began to sob.

"Hey, Annie," Kellan cooed, rubbing her arm. "Are you okay?"

"Yeah." She laughed in spite of herself. "I guess it's silly to be so happy to see my family that I cry, huh?"

"No, it's not. It makes perfect sense. I think your brother was feeling emotional too. He didn't cry, but he looked like he might when we first got there."

"I noticed it too." Anna Mae fished a tissue from the center console and wiped her eyes and nose. She pointed at an approaching intersection. "Turn right here and then take the second left."

"Yes, ma'am." Kellan negotiated the turns. "Where are you taking me?"

"You'll see." Anna Mae rubbed her abdomen as the familiar farmhouse came into view. She directed Kellan to turn onto a long driveway leading to the large home.

Memories flooded her mind—long hot days working in the garden, lazy summer nights spent sitting on the porch singing, winter evenings spent watching the snow from the front windows. Her whole childhood had played out in that very house. Her first Christmas, her first birthday, her first kiss from her childhood friend Daniel Yoder, her first heartbreak when Daniel told her he was in love with Linda Chupp—every significant childhood memory came from that farmhouse.

A light shone from the center window on the second floor. "He's still awake," she mumbled. "Probably reading from the Bible."

"Who?" he asked.

"My father," she whispered.

"Oh. Do you want to go up to the house?"

She shook her head. "No. I don't think he'd want to see me." Fresh tears splattered on her cheeks.

"Come here." He pulled her over to him and kissed the top of her head. "Don't cry. You don't know how tomorrow night is going to turn out. He may see you and break down in tears, realizing how much he missed you."

"I doubt it." She wiped her tears with the tissue.

Kellan rubbed her cheek with his thumb. "His heart will be full of joy when he sees you're carrying another grandchild for him. You mark my words."

A bump came from within her abdomen, and she giggled.

"What?" he asked, a smile growing on his handsome face.

"Feel this." She put his hand over the area where the kicks were plunking her. "I think Butterbean hears her daddy."

Kellan gave a little laugh. "See? Even our Junior agrees with me."

"Junior?" she asked with a chuckle.

"Yes, Junior," he continued. "You just see tomorrow night. His grandpa will be so thrilled to see you that he'll welcome us back into the family. Right, little buddy?" He kissed her and then put the SUV in reverse and backed out of the driveway. "Let's get you back to the room so you can get some rest. Tomorrow will be another exciting day."

Kathryn gently closed the door to Lizzie and Ruthie's room and then crossed the hall. Opening the door, she peeked in and found Junior and Manny snoring in their beds.

She tiptoed down the hallway with a smile and entered the bedroom. "They're all sleeping," she said.

David looked up from his Bible and nodded. "It was a long and exciting night for them," he said, placing the Bible on his bedside table.

Kathryn sat on the edge of the bed and took a deep breath. "Are you still angry with me about the visit?"

He sighed. "I'm still not convinced it's going to go well tomorrow. It was *gut* to see her and Kellan, but I don't think this is the right time."

She gave him a sad smile. "I respect your thoughts, but would you try to keep an open mind tomorrow?"

He shrugged. "I'm not certain it will help. You can't change my father."

"No, I can't, but I can pray." She nodded toward the Bible. "What were you reading?"

"I was reading in Colossians and a Scripture has been echoing in my mind: 'Bear with each other and forgive whatever grievances you may have against one another. Forgive as the Lord forgave you.'" He took her hands in his. "I'll remind my *daed* of that verse if I have to."

Kathryn nodded. "That sounds like a *gut* plan."

He frowned. "I just hope my *daed* listens."

"Have faith." She leaned over and brushed her lips against his. "I do."

CHAPTER 8

The next morning, Anna Mae sat with Kellan at the long table in the formal dining room of the bed and breakfast. Platters of scrambled eggs, bacon, sausage links, buttered toast, and hash browns cluttered the center of the table.

Anna Mae sipped a glass of orange juice and listened as Richard and Sandra Sheppard, the innkeepers, discussed the day's weather. When a knock sounded on the door, Sandra excused herself and headed toward the kitchen.

Filling her plate with eggs and toast, Anna Mae contemplated the day, wondering what her siblings were doing and if she would get a chance to see them. Familiar female voices filled the kitchen, and her heart thumped.

Could it be?

"She's right in here," Sandra said, moving into the doorway to the dining room.

Anna Mae glanced over just as Vera stepped into the doorway and smiled. Fannie and Barbie followed with hesitant expressions.

Anna Mae gasped. *"Mei schweschdern."* Her heart filled with joy.

"Anna Mae!" Vera came toward her with her arms outstretched.

Anna Mae stood and Vera engulfed her in her arms. "It's so good to see you," Anna Mae said. "How did you know we were staying here?"

"Kathryn told me. I went to see her this morning and asked if you'd made it for your visit. You look *wunderbaar gut*!" Vera held her hands. "How are you?" She gestured toward Anna Mae's belly. "When are you due?"

"I'm doing well, and I'm due January fifteen." Anna Mae gestured toward Kellan. "You remember my husband, Kellan." She motioned toward her sisters. "Kellan, you remember Vera, Fannie, and Barbie."

While Fannie and Barbie stood back by the door, Vera held out her hand to him. "How are you?" she asked.

"Fine," he said, shaking her hand. He turned to Fannie and Barbie. "How are you?"

They nodded, muttering *gut* in unison.

Sandra appeared with a tray containing donuts, mugs, and a coffee pot. "Why don't you ladies join Kellan and Anna Mae?" She deposited the tray on the table.

"Thank you," Kellan said.

"We'll let you all visit," Sandra said, moving to the door.

"Please let us know if you need anything," Richard chimed in before following her into the kitchen.

"Thank you so much," Anna Mae said. She then gestured toward the chairs. "Please join us."

Vera sat next to Anna Mae while Fannie and Barbie sank into seats at the end of the table. Kellan poured each of them a cup of coffee.

"How are your children?" Anna Mae asked.

Vera prattled on about each of her seven children, and Anna Mae nodded and smiled. Anna Mae then shared information about her life in Baltimore and her work in Kellan's business and with the quilt ministry. She asked Fannie and Barbie about their families, and they gave her short updates. Anna Mae wished they would warm up to her like Vera had.

"Have you seen *Daed*?" Barbie asked while gripping her mug.

"No, not yet," Anna Mae said. She idly fingered her napkin. "We're having supper with *Mamm* and *Daed* at David's tonight." She glanced over at Kellan, who gave her an encouraging smile.

"Do you think that's a good idea?" Fannie asked, lifting her cup to her mouth.

Anna Mae glanced at Vera. "Well, I . . ."

"I think it's a *wunderbaar* idea," Vera said. "This is the best time of year for a family to get together and work things out."

Barbie and Fannie exchanged looks of disbelief. Ignoring them, Vera updated Anna Mae on community news about friends who lived nearby.

"I would love to see everyone," Anna Mae said. "It would be nice to get the whole family together."

"It's too bad you just missed a church Sunday," Vera said. "That would be a good place to see everyone."

"We could always come back in the spring and plan to be here on a church Sunday," Kellan offered.

Anna Mae nodded. "That would be nice."

They chatted and shared stories for more than two hours.

When Vera glanced at the clock, she stood. "I guess we'd better go. I told Lydia we'd be back by noon. I better call the driver."

"Would you ladies like a ride somewhere?" Kellan offered, standing.

"Oh no," Barbie said. "We can call our driver to come and get us."

"Don't be silly," Kellan said. "Anna Mae can rest for a while, and I can take you back to your house."

Barbie and Fannie exchanged cautious glances and Vera scowled at them. She then smiled at Kellan. "Of course we would like a ride. *Danki*, Kellan."

Anna Mae stood next to Kellan. "I'll ride with you."

"No, you rest." Kellan kissed her forehead. "I'll take them. I'm sure we'll see them again soon. I'm going to run and get my coat and keys. I'll meet you in the kitchen."

Anna Mae's eyes filled with tears as she turned to Vera. "I hate to see you go."

"I promise we'll get together again soon." Vera hugged her. "*Ich liebe dich, mei schweschder*," she whispered.

"I love you too," Anna Mae said, wiping her eyes. She turned to Barbie and Fannie, who gave her uncomfortable smiles. "It was so good to see you both."

"You and your family are in my prayers," Fannie said, touching Anna Mae's hand.

"*Ya*," Barbie said with a nod. "May God bless you and your family."

Anna Mae followed them to the door where they met Kellan. She waved as they hurried off toward the truck. Tears trickled down her cheeks while she headed back into her room. It was wonderful to spend time with her sisters, but the cold manner in which Fannie and Barbie treated her was painful. Of course she'd expected it, but she'd hoped all of her siblings would've been warm like Vera and Kathryn.

Lying down on the bed, she hoped for a miracle, that her parents would receive her warmly too.

Anna Mae grasped Kellan's hand while they walked up the path to Kathryn's house later that evening. Her heart skittered with a mixture of anxiety and excitement when they reached the door. Taking a deep breath, she knocked and then pushed the door open to find her nieces and nephews gathered around her parents.

When her gaze met her mother's, Mary Rose stood and gasped. "Is that you, Anna Mae?" she asked in *Dietsch*. "Is this my Anna Mae?"

Anna Mae nodded. "*Ya*, it's me, *Mamm*. It's really me. Kellan and I came to see you for Christmas." She turned to her father and found him staring at her, a deep frown imprinted on his face.

Mary Rose rushed to the door. "Oh, my! It's a *Grischtdaag* miracle!" She gathered Anna Mae in her arms and wept. "God has answered my most fervent prayers."

"*Mamm*," Anna Mae whispered, her voice quavering. "It's so good to see you. I've missed you so much." Her mother smelled just as she'd remembered—vanilla mixed with strawberry.

"Oh, Anna Mae," Mary Rose said, taking her face in her

hands. "Let me look at you." She glanced down and gasped again. "You're expecting!"

"*Ya,*" Anna Mae said. "It's our first."

"When are you due?" Mary Rose asked.

"January fifteen." She smiled at Kellan.

He held out his hand. "Mrs. Beiler, it's so good to see you. You look well."

"Oh, Kellan!" Mary Rose shook his hand. "Are you taking *gut* care of my *dochder?*"

"Yes, ma'am." Kellan looped his arm around Anna Mae's shoulders and beamed. "She's the light of my life. I'm so blessed to have her by my side."

Kathryn entered the room and rushed over to them. "Kellan! Anna Mae!" She held out her hands. "Hand me your coats, and let's head into the kitchen. Supper is ready. I made my famous meatloaf and rolls."

"It smells wonderful," Kellan said, handing her his coat. He then helped Anna Mae out of her wrap.

"*Kinner,*" Kathryn called. "Go wash up and then get to the table. It's time to eat."

The children filed out of the room with Kathryn in tow.

Mary Rose squeezed Anna Mae's shoulders. "I've prayed for you every day since you left. Oh, you must tell me everything about your life in Baltimore."

"Of course." Anna Mae glanced over at her father and found him still scowling at her. With trembling legs, she cleared her throat and stepped over to him. "*Daed,*" she said. "It's *gut* to see you. You look well."

Still glowering, he studied her, but said nothing in response.

"Sir," Kellan said, holding out his hand. "It's a pleasure to see you again."

Daed grunted and looked back at Anna Mae. "You will cover your head in this house. It's only proper." He turned to Mary Rose. "I will not eat at the same table as her." He stood and marched toward the kitchen.

Anna Mae cupped a hand to her mouth to stifle a gasp. She then closed her eyes and took deep breaths to stop her threatening tears. When she opened her eyes again, she found her mother and Kellan studying her.

"This was a mistake," Anna Mae whispered. "I never should've come." She met Kellan's concerned gaze. "You were right. I don't belong here."

"No, no. Don't say that. It's going to be okay," Mary Rose said quickly. "Your father is just hurt that you left, but he still loves you. Kathryn has a kerchief you can borrow. Your *daed* will come around. Just do as he asks, and everything will be okay. We can set up a small table in the kitchen for you and Kellan. It will be just fine." Her eyes pleaded with Anna Mae's. "Please don't leave. You just got here. I want to visit with you and get to know you again."

"I won't leave," Anna Mae said. "I promise."

"*Gut.*" Mary Rose headed out of the room. "I'll be right back."

Anna Mae turned to Kellan. "This was much worse than I thought. I never should've come here." Her voice was thick. "I thought for sure he would forgive me, but he won't. Did you see his eyes?" She sniffed as tears welled up in her eyes.

"Shh." Kellan placed a finger on her lips. "This wasn't a mistake. You've answered your mother's prayers, Annie.

You're supposed to be here. Your father may take a little longer to reach, but we have a few more days. Just give him time and trust God."

"I have a kerchief for you." Mary Rose appeared with a head covering. "Let me put this on you." She put the blue material over Anna Mae's head and tied it under her chin. "Now, let's go eat as a family."

Anna Mae and Kellan followed Mary Rose into the kitchen, where the family was gathered around the large table. In the corner was a smaller table with two chairs and place settings. Anna Mae glanced up at Kellan, who gave a tentative smile.

"It's okay," he whispered. "Just do as your father asks, and he'll come around." He took her hand and gently pulled her toward the table.

Anna Mae sank into a chair at the small table with Kellan sitting across from her. They followed her relatives' lead and bowed their heads in silent prayer, and Kellan took her hands in his. With her eyes closed, she silently thanked God for the many blessings in her life and asked Him to work on her father's heart.

When she heard the utensils hitting the dishes, she looked up and found the family filling their plates. Anna Mae turned toward the table and studied her parents. They looked exactly as she'd remembered them, except for maybe a few more wrinkles on their faces. Henry was still a brooding man with graying brown hair and a matching beard, while Mary Rose still had striking brown eyes and graying light brown hair peeking out from under her prayer *kapp*.

Kathryn rose and brought a platter of meatloaf, potatoes, and green beans over to Anna Mae and Kellan.

"I'm sorry about this little table," Kathryn muttered. "I tried to talk Henry out of it, but he insisted you sit over here."

Anna Mae forced a smile. "I expected it but had hoped for something more inviting." She filled her plate with the meatloaf.

"I'll sit with you." Kathryn frowned. "I think it's wrong for you to be here alone, and I don't care about the rules. You're my family."

"No." Anna Mae touched her hand. "I don't want to be the cause of problems between you and David."

Kathryn stuck out her chin. "I refuse to treat you like an outsider." She stepped over to the table and whispered something to David, who stared at her, frowning.

"She means business, huh?" Kellan whispered with a smile.

"Kathryn has always been known for speaking her mind and standing up for her convictions, sometimes to the chagrin of my brother," Anna Mae replied.

Kathryn returned, carrying a chair. She grabbed a dish and utensils from the adjacent table and then seated herself next to Anna Mae. "Your brother isn't too happy with me, but he'll have to get over it," she said. "You came to visit and I'm going to spend time with you."

Anna Mae glanced toward the table and found her mother smiling at her. She moved her eyes to her father, who continued to frown. Feeling a lump swelling in her throat, Anna Mae studied her glass of water.

Kathryn filled her plate with food. "Tell me what you did today."

"I had a surprise this morning," Anna Mae said. "My sisters came to see me at the bed and breakfast."

"Oh." Kathryn grinned. "What a nice surprise."

"Thank you for telling them where we're staying," Anna Mae said while filling her fork with meatloaf.

"*Gern gschehne,*" Kathryn said. "How was your visit with them?"

Anna Mae explained how Vera was warm and Fannie and Barbie were cold.

Kathryn shook her head. "I'm sorry about that. They behaved the same way when I mentioned you might visit, and I'd hoped that Fannie and Barbie had come around. Still, it speaks volumes that they came to see you. That's a step in the right direction." She turned the conversation to the threat of a blizzard while they finished their meal.

After supper, David came over to their table. After giving Kathryn a hard look, he nodded at Anna Mae. "It's *gut* to see you." He then turned to Kellan. "Would you like to join me in the barn? It's sort of a tradition for men to stand around and chat after a meal, even in the cold weather."

Kellan glanced at Anna Mae, who smiled in response. He then looked at David. "Sure." He kissed Anna Mae on the head before following David out of the kitchen.

Glancing around, Anna Mae found that Henry had left the kitchen, and she assumed that he had already gone outside. The voices of her young nieces and nephews rose from the family room where they were playing games.

Anna Mae rose and began to pick up the plates.

"Don't be *narrisch*," Kathryn said, touching her hand. "I don't expect you to do dishes in your condition."

"I'm pregnant, not bedridden," Anna Mae said, carrying dishes to the sink.

Kathryn shook her head. "You may sit and watch me do the dishes, but you will not help. I won't hear of it." She turned to Mary Rose. "You sit with her and visit while Amanda and I do the dishes. You two have a lot of catching up to do."

Mary Rose sat across from Anna Mae and held her hands. "Tell me everything about Baltimore. Are you *froh*?"

Anna Mae smiled and nodded. "*Ya*, I am." She then told her mother all about her quilting ministry at the church and about her job working in the office at the dealership. She asked about her siblings, nieces, and nephews, and Mary Rose told her how they each were doing.

Mary Rose was in the middle of sharing a funny story about one of her nephews when Henry came through the door.

Avoiding eye contact with Anna Mae, he frowned at his wife. "It's time to go, Mary Rose," he grumbled. He started toward the door and then turned back to her. "Now."

Mary Rose's eyes were wide with shock. "Henry, do you see your youngest *dochder* sitting here? Don't you want to speak with her?"

He kept his eyes fixed on Mary Rose. "I said it's time to go. I'll be out front waiting for you in the buggy."

"Henry!" Mary Rose called after him. She turned to Anna Mae. "I'm sorry. I have to go."

"But, *Mamm*," Anna Mae began. "I came all this way to see you."

"I know." Mary Rose stood. "But you know your father." She hugged Kathryn. "Supper was *wunderbaar. Danki*." She then touched Anna Mae's shoulder. "Come and visit me before you leave."

Anna Mae stood with tears in her eyes. "You can't let him do this to me, *Mamm*. Kellan and I were hoping that we could be a family again. You have to stand up to *Daed*."

"He's the bishop." Mary Rose's eyes filled with tears. "I have to go. *Ich liebe dich, mei dochder*." She patted Anna Mae's hand and then rushed out of the kitchen.

"*Mamm! Mamm!*" Anna Mae started after her. "Please don't go."

"Anna Mae!" Kathryn grabbed Anna Mae's arm and pulled her back to the table. "Stop. Just let her go."

"What if I never see her again?" Anna Mae lowered herself into the chair.

"Shh." Kathryn sat beside her and rubbed her arm. "Trust God to heal the family."

Covering her face with her hands, Anna Mae dissolved into tears.

❧

David leaned against the barn door and glanced up toward the sky. Large flurries twirled and danced to the ground, covering the pasture with a silver quilt. He glanced over at his English brother-in-law, who shivered and hugged his arms to his lanky body. "I hope you packed a warmer coat because I heard we're supposed to have a white Christmas this year," David said.

The door opened and slammed, and Henry marched down the porch steps.

"Here's *Daed*." David sent an uneasy glance Kellan's way as Henry moved toward them. "*Daed*, would you like to join—?"

"David, help me get my horse hitched up," Henry said, pushing past him into the barn.

David glanced at Kellan, who shrugged.

"*Daed*?" David followed him into the barn. "You're leaving?"

"*Ya*, I am." Henry led his horse from the stall. "I'd appreciate your help getting the horse readied."

David placed his hand on his arm to stop him. "Why are you going?"

Henry narrowed his eyes. "I think you know why." He pushed past David with the horse in tow.

David followed him out of the barn toward the buggy. "Why can't you stay and visit?"

Henry glanced at Kellan on his way to the buggy. "You know why." He hitched the horse to the buggy.

David glanced at Kellan and found him scowling.

"It's all right," David said. "I'll talk to him."

"There's no need to talk to me," Henry said. "I've already told your *mamm* to come out here so we can go home."

"You can't do that to *Mamm*," David said. "Didn't you see *Mamm's* face when she saw Anna Mae was here? This means so much to her. Taking her away from Anna Mae is wrong."

Henry faced him, shaking a finger in his face. "It's not your place to tell me what's right and what's wrong."

David threw his hands up in frustration. "Anna Mae made her decision to leave and was shunned. But you and I both know that shunning tradition dictates that we can't eat at the same table as she does and we can't conduct business with her. It says nothing about visiting with her, which is what we were doing in the house." He gestured toward the house. "Leaving isn't necessary, and it's not right to do that to *Mamm* or Anna Mae."

"You have no right to judge me, son." Henry finished hitching the horse and glanced toward the house. "It's written: 'for all have sinned and fall short of the glory of God, and are justified freely by his grace through the redemption that came by Christ Jesus.'"

David narrowed his eyes, challenging him. "What about that verse in Colossians: 'Bear with each other and forgive whatever grievances you may have against one another. Forgive as the Lord forgave you.'"

"Where's your *mamm*?" Henry asked, keeping his eyes averted from David's stare.

"You should go without her," David said, resentment bubbling up inside him. "I'll bring her home or she can stay here tonight."

"You stay out of this." Henry started toward the house. "I'll go find her."

David turned and found Kellan standing alone, his face rigid.

"I'm so sorry," David apologized. "I don't understand why he's making more of this than it is." David leaned against

110

the barn door and watched the snowflakes land on the fence posts. "Anna Mae made her choice and he's not going to change that. It's obvious that you and Anna Mae are happy."

Kellan spoke slowly. "I know it was risky to come here, but Anna Mae really wanted to see her family again. I just hope this doesn't break her heart." He gave a slight nod toward the porch where Mary Rose and Henry were descending the steps. "I'll stay here until they've left," he said. "I don't want to cause any more trouble."

David stepped over toward his parents, and the hurt and sadness in his mother's eyes nearly broke his heart.

Before speaking in *Dietsch*, David took a deep breath, hoping to calm his frayed nerves. "You don't have to leave, *Daed*. No one will think less of you as a bishop if you visit with Anna Mae."

Mary Rose gave Henry a hopeful look, while Henry kept his eyes trained on the horse.

"I cannot stay here," Henry declared before climbing into the buggy.

David frowned, but he knew from his father's tone of voice that arguing would do no good. Bending down, he hugged Mary Rose. "I'm sorry the evening had to end this way," he whispered to her. "Kathryn had hoped that *Daed* would see the visit as an opportunity to mend the family."

"It's not your fault," she whispered. "Your *daed* is a stubborn old mule. *Gut nacht*." She then climbed into the buggy.

David stood alone as they rode off through the swirling flurries.

Anna Mae wiped her cheeks with a napkin. "I guess I was wrong to think my coming here would be a joyous reunion with my parents."

"No, you weren't wrong." Kathryn's eyes were full of concern. "I thought your *daed* would be so overwhelmed with happiness to see you that he would welcome you with a hug and a prayer of thanksgiving."

Anna Mae shook her head. "It's no use. He won't ever accept me."

"Don't say that." Kathryn rubbed Anna Mae's shoulder. "God will change his mind. I can feel it."

Kellan burst into the room, rushed to the table, and crouched beside Anna Mae. "Are you okay?" He took her hand in his.

Anna Mae nodded. "I'm fine. Just disappointed." The worry in his eyes caused hers to tear up again.

"I don't know what your father was saying in that Pennsylvania Dutch, but I could tell he was angry that we were here." He shook his head. "It doesn't make sense to me. You came to visit him, and he left in a huff."

"He's hurt that she left the faith," Kathryn said. "It's painful for a parent when the child leaves the community."

Kellan shook his head. "She was a grown woman and it was her choice. I didn't want to steal her away. I left it up to her, and she chose me."

"Let's not go through this all again," Anna Mae said. "What's done is done, and I let him and the rest of my family and the community down. I thought that by coming here we could work things out, but he couldn't stand to stay in the same house with me. He didn't want my mother to stay either. I couldn't convince her to stay and visit with me. She followed him outside."

"We should go home." Kellan stood. "We'll go back to the bed and breakfast and pack up our things."

"No," Anna Mae said with more force than she'd planned. "I can't give up now. I'm already here."

Kellan placed a hand on her abdomen. "But the baby. The stress your father is causing could hurt the baby."

"I'm feeling fine. I've been resting, so there's nothing to worry about." Anna Mae averted her eyes by staring at the wood grain of the table.

Kellan put a hand on her shoulder. "We should go home and plan to visit later, after the baby is here. Maybe next spring. The weather will be better and you and the baby will be ready to travel." He took her hand and lifted her to her feet. "Let's go say goodbye to everyone and head home."

Kathryn touched Kellan's shoulder. "Don't give up on Henry yet. He's a stubborn man, but he has a deep faith in God. Give him a chance to adjust to seeing you and Anna Mae together."

Kellan raked his hand through his brown hair and turned to Anna Mae.

She studied his eyes and silently prayed he'd agree with Kathryn. "We've come all this way," she whispered, taking his hands in hers. "Won't you give him another chance?"

"Give him another day," Kathryn said. "If it doesn't work out, then David and I will come and visit you this spring."

"You will?" Anna Mae smiled as joy filled her heart. "You'll come see us?"

"*Ya*, we will," she said. "David had suggested that we visit you this spring instead of you coming here for Christmas."

"Oh, that would be lovely!" Anna Mae hugged her. "We'd love to have you visit, right, Kellan?"

Kellan nodded. "Anytime you want to come, you're welcome in our home."

"I hope I didn't get you in too much trouble with David by coming out for Christmas," Anna Mae said. "I hate that you went against his wishes."

Kathryn shrugged. "It wasn't the first time that I followed my heart instead of David's suggestions."

Anna Mae laughed. "No, it certainly wasn't."

Kathryn's expression became serious. "Join us for lunch at your parents' house tomorrow at noon, and we'll try one more time. If it doesn't work out, then we'll take it from there. You've come too far to give up this easily."

"Lunch at my parents' house?" Anna Mae asked. "Who will be there?"

"Just David and our immediate family," Kathryn explained. "It's our turn with them since the rest of David's siblings planned to see them on other days to have their Christmas celebrations. You know how hectic it gets this time of year. We put our word in for Christmas Eve first."

Anna Mae nodded and let the words process. Christmas Eve with her parents. She could be strong; she could do this. She turned to Kellan. "Does that sound okay to you? We'll try lunch tomorrow."

Kellan sighed. "I'll go along with it on one condition."

Anna Mae nodded. "What's your condition?"

He put a fingertip under her chin and angled her face so

that she was staring directly into his warm eyes. "I won't stay here if the stress is too much for you and our baby. If things take a turn for the worse, then we will leave. Do you agree with me?"

Overwhelmed by the love in his eyes, Anna Mae nodded as more tears filled her eyes. "Yes," she whispered.

"Then we have a deal." He kissed the top of her head. "I'll let you ladies talk a few minutes while I go say goodbye to your brother. We shouldn't stay too late. You and the baby need your rest." He then headed out of the kitchen.

"He really loves you," Kathryn said.

Anna Mae sighed. "I just wish my father would see that."

David hung up his coat and blew out a sigh. Turning, he spotted Kellan coming from the kitchen. "How is Anna Mae?" he asked.

"As well as can be expected," Kellan said. "May I talk to you a minute?"

David waved his hand toward the quiet family room. The children had gone upstairs to get ready for bed. Sinking into a rocker, David patted the chair next to him. "Have a seat."

"Don't mind if I do." Kellan lowered himself onto the chair and jammed his hands in his pockets. "What a night, huh?"

David kept his eyes fixed on the flames crackling in the fireplace. "*Ya*, I reckon it has been."

"There's something I need to ask you," Kellan said.

David faced him. "What is it?"

"I didn't understand much of what your dad said out by

the barn earlier since he was speaking Pennsylvania Dutch. But, at the same time, I'm not stupid. From what I deduced, he wants Annie and me to leave, right?" Kellan's expression was serious but also sad.

Suddenly David felt as if he'd been transported back in time. Once again, he was trapped in the middle between his father's strict Amish ways and Anna Mae's choice to leave the community.

"You don't have to sugarcoat it, David," Kellan continued. "I'll take it like a man."

"My father wasn't happy you and Anna Mae were here," David began, facing him. "He didn't say that he wanted you to leave, but he did say he couldn't stay here."

"I told Annie that we should go home, but she's insisting on staying through tomorrow to see if she can smooth it over." Kellan shook his head, frowning. "I'm concerned the visit is going to be too stressful if it keeps going the way it is. While the doctor said that it was safe for us to make this trip, I'm worried the stress of all of this might hurt her or the baby."

David absently rubbed his beard as worry filled him. "I hadn't thought about that."

Kellan leaned back on the chair. "I just don't understand it. How can a father treat his child that way? It doesn't make sense to me. Annie made her choice when she married me and it was *her* choice. I didn't force her to leave your community. In fact, I asked her several times if she was certain she wanted to give up this life for me, and every time I asked, she insisted she was."

"I knew that *Daed* would have trouble welcoming Anna

Mae," David said. "I warned Kathryn, but she insisted on arranging this visit."

Kellan shook his head and held his hands palms up. "I don't understand it. Annie and I have been married almost three years. We're expecting our first child and we're happy. She's everything to me and she tells me I'm everything to her. She's not coming back here or going to join your church again, but she wants to be a part of the Beiler family. Why can't Henry accept that?"

David shook his head. "I don't think you understand my father's point of view. He was deeply hurt when Anna Mae left. We know that once a member of the community has left, it's rare that she comes back, and it's devastating for the parents. On top of that, it's more complicated than that for my father. He's the bishop, and I'm certain he feels like he failed as a father and leader of the church because she chose to leave."

"How is he a failure?" Kellan said. "He should be proud of his daughter. Anna Mae is a good wife and will be a wonderful mother too. She may live and worship God in a different way than the way she was raised, but all the most important elements of her faith are still there. The rest is just window dressing."

David nodded. "I see your point, but I also see my father's. It's not an easy situation at all."

Kellan sighed. "It just kills me to see Annie so upset. She came here with the best of intentions." He glanced at his watch. "I'm going to see if she's ready to head back to the room. I want to be sure she gets her sleep." He stood and headed into the kitchen.

David watched him leave, rubbing his beard in frustration. It was obvious that Kellan was a good Christian man who cared for his sister. But would his father ever acknowledge that fact?

He sighed and got up to poke at the fire. He'd done all he could. Now he had to leave the rest up to God.

CHAPTER 9

Mary Rose sat on the edge of the bed while thoughts of her beautiful Anna Mae swirled through her mind. How could Henry rebuff their daughter? Of course Mary Rose understood the importance of shunning, but Henry had gone way beyond what was expected of an Amish person, even a bishop. His behavior had been downright cruel, and it broke her heart to see Anna Mae so distraught.

Her eyes moved to the other side of the bedroom where Henry changed into his nightclothes. His silence had been deafening since they'd climbed into the buggy at David's house. It was bad enough that he'd insisted they leave David's home soon after supper, but the way he sat in silence after the incident was the icing on the cake. Resentment and disappointment surged within her.

"Go ahead and say it, Mary Rose," he grumbled, pulling on his nightshirt. "I know you're waiting to speak your mind."

"I don't understand you," she whispered, angry tears spilling down her cheeks. "Your youngest *dochder* comes back to see you and tell you that she's expecting her first *boppli*, and you treat her like an enemy. How could you, Henry Beiler?"

"You know the position I'm in as bishop." He crossed the room and climbed into bed.

She swiped her hand across her wet cheeks. "*Ya*, I do, but I also know you're a *gut daed* and a *gut* man. I expected you to treat her with love and respect, despite the fact that she left us. She's still our *dochder* no matter where she lives or whom she chooses as her husband. Kellan McDonough is a *gut* man, and he'll be a *gut daed*. We need to accept him as well as our *dochder* or we'll lose her and her *boppli*. Is that what you want? Do you want to lose Anna Mae altogether?"

"She made her choice when she left," he said, rolling onto his side and facing the wall.

"I want to be a part of her life." Mary Rose stood and crossed to his side of the bed. "You can't take her away from me."

"I'm sure you're just as hurt as I am that she left."

"Have you no heart, Henry?" Her voice shook with resentment. "Have you no feelings for your own *kinner*?"

"I never said I didn't love her," he muttered. "She left me. I mean, she left us, all of us. Our whole family. She hurt us all when she rejected us."

"That's not true. She never rejected us, Henry. She simply chose another life, but she's still our *dochder*."

His eyes closed and a snore escaped his chest.

"Don't you fall asleep on me!" Mary Rose's voice shook with renewed anger. "This conversation is not over, Henry. I want our *dochder* to be a part of our *Grischtdaag*, and you can't stop that." Turning, she stomped from the bedroom and down to the family room, where she curled up on the sofa and opened her Bible. Taking a deep breath, she prayed for guidance on how to deal with her stubborn husband.

While her eyes scanned the many verses, she thought of her beautiful Anna Mae. How her heart had swelled when she'd first laid eyes on her youngest *dochder*. While she'd never quite overcome the hurt and disappointment that Anna Mae had left to marry an Englisher, she felt at peace after seeing her again. Before she saw her father's rejection, Anna Mae's face had shone with happiness and joy.

And she was going to be a *mamm*! What a *wunderbaar* miracle!

Mary Rose could not understand why Henry was being so cruel to Anna Mae. He'd have been acting within the rules if he'd visited with their *dochder* and her husband for a few hours before they'd gone home.

Mary Rose let Henry's words turn over in her mind. He'd said that Anna Mae had hurt everyone when she'd rejected them. Was Henry nursing a broken heart? Could that be the reason for his anger toward Anna Mae?

Shaking her head with confusion and disgust, Mary Rose glanced back down at the Bible. She read along, trying to put her resentment out of her mind and concentrate on the Lord's Word.

A Scripture caught her eye, and she whispered it aloud, "Ephesians 4:2: Be completely humble and gentle; be patient, bearing with one another in love." She allowed the words to sink into her heart.

Why couldn't Henry remember this verse when he was with Anna Mae tonight? Henry should've remembered to be patient, humble, and gentle with their daughter. She was just as precious as their other children, even though she was no longer Amish.

Mary Rose stared at the verse until it struck her: she too needed to be gentle and patient, bearing with her husband in love even though she was exasperated by his stubbornness and hurt by his actions. Still, questions tumbled through her mind. She wanted to understand Henry's behavior, and she also longed to know how she could help him change.

While she loved Henry with all her heart, she couldn't let him hurt their daughter this way. Mary Rose was determined to have Anna Mae back in her life. She wanted to know and love her youngest grandchild. She needed more time with Anna Mae, and she needed to find a way to get it before it was too late.

She closed the Bible and set it on the end table. Then she lowered herself onto her side on the sofa and draped a quilt over her body. She recited her evening prayers, adding an extra one for Henry, asking the Lord to warm his heart toward their youngest child. She then asked God to keep Anna Mae in town long enough for Mary Rose to visit with her and bond with her.

Drifting off to sleep, Mary Rose dreamed that she was sitting on a porch with Anna Mae and her newborn child, laughing and chatting while the warm sun shone down on them.

Kathryn tiptoed down the hallway from Manny's room toward her bedroom. Stepping through the doorway, she found David staring out the window. Taking a deep breath, she walked over to him, hoping he wouldn't be angry with her for the incidents that had unfolded this evening.

"I'm sorry things didn't go better tonight with your *dat*," Kathryn said, crossing her arms over her chest. "You were right, and I was wrong to defy you. I was also foolish to assume that things would go smoothly."

"I was right about my father." Turning, he faced her, frowning. "And to make it worse, you put me in a bad position when you ate with her and Kellan."

Kathryn shrugged. "She's still family whether she's shunned or not."

"But you know the rules as well as I do. Your defiance doesn't reflect well on me or this family." He sighed. "I too had hoped things would've gone better."

She raised an eyebrow. "Are you saying I was right about having Anna Mae and Kellan visit?"

"I didn't say that," he began. "It was a disaster at best, and I'm still angry and hurt that you planned this behind my back. However, I do think it's time we tried to bring the family back together."

Kathryn suppressed a smile. David was finally starting to see things her way.

"Anna Mae's heart was in the right place, but the plan to reunite the Beiler family for *Grischtdaag* didn't work." Shaking his head, he frowned. "I don't think my *daed* can get over his hurt that quickly. She's the youngest, the baby. Imagine how we would feel if Manny left."

"I hope your *daed* gets over it soon because it's killing your *mamm*." She took his hand in hers.

He rubbed his beard, his brown eyes deep in thought. "I changed my mind about Kellan tonight."

"What do you mean?" Still holding his warm hands in hers, she led him to the bed, where they sat.

"He's a *gut* man and clearly loves my sister. We talked and it was obvious that he loves God and takes good care of Anna Mae." He shook his head. "I wish my father could see that. Maybe then he would accept them both as part of the family."

"All is not lost." Kathryn squeezed his hands in hers. "I've asked Anna Mae to join us at your parents' house tomorrow and we can try again."

David shook his head. "You should give up this idea of a Christmas miracle. It won't work."

"*Ya*, it will." She nodded with emphasis. "Didn't you see the joy in your *mamm's* eyes when she first saw Anna Mae? That was all I needed to see to know I made the right choice. Anna Mae was meant to come here. It's God's will."

David stood and walked over toward the window again. "I don't know, Katie. I don't think it's our place to decide God's will. My *daed* is going to become even angrier when he finds out Anna Mae and Kellan are still here. I'm certain he thinks that they headed home tonight. He'll be less than pleased if they show up for Christmas Eve lunch. He'll blow his top and possibly not speak to you or me for a very long time."

"Don't say that." Kathryn crossed the room to him. "Don't you believe in *Grischtdaag* miracles, David?" She placed her hand on his shoulder. "Remember our first *Grischtdaag* together as husband and wife when I told you we were going to have Amanda? That was a miracle."

"But this is different," David said. He stared out the window. "This isn't about having a child. This is about working out family differences. These problems run deep and can't be solved by sharing a dinner and telling the *Grischtdaag* story."

"Look at me." She cupped his face in her hands and turned it toward her. The worry in his deep brown eyes broke her heart. "I need you to trust me that this is going to work out. I need you to believe in a *Grischtdaag* miracle for the sake of our family. Please, David. For me."

A sad smile turned up the corners of his lips. "Your faith never ceases to amaze me, Katie. But this goes beyond your belief in signs and miracles. I don't think that there is an easy fix to this. I can't tell you that I believe in *Grischtdaag* miracles."

She sighed and ran her finger down his cheek. "I hope to prove you wrong, David Beiler, because I believe that there will be a miracle."

He nodded. "I hope you're right and I'm wrong."

Lounging on the bed in their room, Anna Mae rubbed her abdomen while watching a news reporter highlight details of a snowstorm that was headed toward Lancaster County that evening.

"Looks like we're going to get hit with quite a bit of snow," Kellan said, sinking onto the bed next to her. "It's a good thing we brought the SUV and not the car." He held up a plate of cookies he'd received from the innkeepers. "Want one?"

"No, thanks." Anna Mae cupped a hand to her mouth to

stifle a yawn. "I don't think I could eat another bite. Things with my dad ruined my appetite. I still can't believe how badly the evening went. I never imagined it would be that bad, but I guess I was kidding myself."

Reaching over, he touched her hand. "I'm sorry that things haven't worked out the way you'd planned. We can always go home tomorrow. If we leave early enough in the day, we'll still be able to enjoy Christmas Eve at home. I can light the fireplace and—"

"No." She shook her head, her eyes filling with tears. "Kathryn invited us for Christmas Eve lunch, and we have to go. I can't go home without giving my dad one more chance. After all, we came all this way. We've already discussed this. Why are you changing your mind now?"

"Okay, okay." He rubbed her arm. "I didn't mean to distress you. We'll try once more, but if your father upsets you again, then we'll head home. I can't stand to watch you grieve. It's too much for me."

She nodded, wiping her eyes. "I promise I'll leave if he upsets me, but you have to let me try once more."

"I will." He smiled. "I just want you to be happy. You know that." He placed the plate on the bedside table and then crossed to the window. Pushing back the shade, he glanced out. "Yup, it's snowing all right. I think we may have a full-fledged blizzard by morning."

Anna Mae opened her mouth to speak, but pressure like fire gripped her abdomen and lower back, stealing her breath. She gasped and clutched her belly.

"Annie?" Kellan rushed to her, dropping onto his knees in front of her. "Are you all right? Do you think labor is starting?"

She shook her head as the pain subsided. Taking deep breaths, she closed her eyes.

He held her hands. "Annie, let me call a doctor." He stood, but she latched onto his hand and pulled him back.

"I'm okay," she whispered, forcing a smile. "Probably false labor. If they're real labor pains, they'll get more regular. After all, I'm not due for three weeks."

A frown twisted Kellan's handsome face. "I think we should go home and you should see Dr. Trask."

"Sit." She pulled him down next to her on the bed and arranged the blankets around them. "Even if we went home, no one would see me unless my labor pains were coming every fifteen minutes." She smiled, his concern warming her soul. "There's no reason to rush home."

"As usual, you win." He kissed her forehead. "But you tell me if the pain gets worse and more frequent. If you start to feel bad, we will go home, Mrs. McDonough."

She snuggled up next to him and placed her head on his muscular chest. "Yes, Mr. McDonough." Closing her eyes, she sighed. "Good night, Kellan."

He encircled her with his arms. "Good night, Annie."

CHAPTER 10

Kathryn stepped into her mother-in-law's kitchen the following morning. The sound of her children's voices filled the room as they ran through the kitchen playing tag and laughing. Mary Rose stood by the stove, pulling out pots and pans.

Kathryn took a deep breath and hoped her plan would go well for lunch. Anna Mae and Kellan would arrive at noon as surprise guests.

Kathryn kissed Mary Rose's cheek. "Can you believe it's Christmas Eve already? Where did the year go?"

"*Ya*," Mary Rose muttered, frowning. "The year has flown by."

Kathryn's heart filled with sadness. "*Was iss letz?*" she asked even though she already knew the answer. "It's about Anna Mae, isn't it?" she whispered.

Mary Rose glanced around the kitchen and moved closer to Kathryn. "I didn't sleep much last night." Her cheeks flushed with embarrassment. "Henry and I had words and I slept on the sofa. He's still not speaking to me."

Dread filled Kathryn's gut. She'd prayed over and over last night and this morning that this dinner would go well and the family could finally begin to heal.

"Let's sit and talk." Kathryn took Mary Rose's hand and led her to the table. "I was worried after you left so abruptly."

Mary Rose sighed. "I was so excited to see Anna Mae. Having her back was an answer to my prayers, and seeing her pregnant was even more *wunderbaar*." She scowled. "I never expected Henry to be so harsh. I expected him to be upset, but for him to drag me away from her was too much. I was so angry and disappointed last night. We both said some terrible things to each other. I couldn't stand to be in the same room with him, so I went downstairs and read my Bible for a while. Then I fell asleep on the sofa. This morning he barely said a word to me. I know he's upset, but I am too. I'm not going to act like nothing happened."

"I'm so sorry, *Mamm*." Kathryn shook her head. "I never meant for Anna Mae's visit to cause so many problems."

Mary Rose's expression became curious. "I keep thinking about the conversation we had in the bakery that day when I told you about how much I missed Anna Mae. It seems too coincidental that she came for *Grischtdaag* after we talked. Did you have something to do with Anna Mae's visit?"

Kathryn studied Mary Rose's hopeful eyes. She knew that the best answer would be the truth, but she hoped it wouldn't upset Mary Rose even more. "If I told you that I did, would you be angry with me?"

"No, no!" Mary Rose shook her head with emphasis. "I would thank you. You helped answer my prayers."

"But is her visit more of a burden than a blessing?" Kathryn touched Mary Rose's hands.

"Oh, of course it is a blessing, Kathryn. You brought my *dochder* back into my life after three long years," Mary Rose said. "No, it didn't cause problems; it just brought to light what I already knew: that I have accepted Anna Mae's decision to leave, and Henry has not. This is something he and I may never agree upon." She tilted her head in question. "Tell me, how did the visit come about? Did you contact Anna Mae after you spoke with me?"

Kathryn shook her head. "No, actually, Anna Mae had contacted me before you and I spoke. She wrote me a letter about a month ago and asked if she could visit. I offered to help her coordinate the details, but I worried that it might not be a good idea because of how Henry could react. I prayed about it and asked God to lead me and use me as He saw fit. What you told me was the sign from God I needed to help Anna Mae plan out the details."

"Did David know?" Mary Rose asked.

Nodding, Kathryn grimaced. "*Ya*, but he was worried that things would go badly. I planned it all behind his back. He was upset when he found out I went on with the plans without his blessing. He and I don't see eye-to-eye about it, but we'll get past it."

Mary Rose's eyes filled with tears. "Tell me, has Anna Mae left to go home?"

Kathryn shook her head. She looked around the kitchen, and finding it empty, she leaned closer to Mary Rose and lowered her voice. "She's still here, and she and Kellan plan to join us for our Christmas Eve meal. However, it's a secret, and I don't think we should share it with *Daed*."

"I won't tell Henry." Mary Rose's eyes filled with excitement as tears trickled down her cheeks. "I'm so thankful that she didn't go home. Last night I prayed that I would see her again. I need more time to visit with her. A few hours weren't nearly enough. I've missed her so much."

"I know you have." Kathryn squeezed her hands. "And she wants more time with you. She was so disappointed when you left."

"I don't understand Henry." Grabbing a napkin, Mary Rose swiped her eyes and nose. "He told me that Anna Mae hurt us all when she left. I would bet she broke his heart, but he hasn't admitted it aloud yet. He needs to heal, not hold onto this anger he's been harboring for the past few years."

Kathryn nodded. "You're right."

"Last night I read my Bible and came across a verse that really spoke to me," Mary Rose continued. "It said: 'Be completely humble and gentle; be patient, bearing with one another in love.' I'm trying to be patient with him, but it's hard."

Kathryn gave a sad smile. "I truly believe God won't give up on Henry. He'll see us through this, and our family will be reunited."

"I hope so." Mary Rose sighed.

Kathryn stood. "We'd better start dinner before we run out of time."

"*Danki.*" Mary Rose pulled her into a hug. "You're a *wunderbaar dochder* and a *wunderbaar fraa* to my David."

"You know I'd do anything for our family," Kathryn said. She stepped over to the counter and grabbed the cookbook. Flipping through the pages, she sent up a silent prayer that dinner would go better today than it had last night.

Anna Mae rubbed her abdomen while Kellan steered the

SUV through the winding streets in the blowing snow. The street was a solid sheet of white, lined with trees donned with white powder, reminding her of garland. Her stomach somersaulted as the vehicle approached her parents' house. The whitewashed clapboard house stood like an apparition in the blowing snow. The roof was pure white, as were the lawn and walkway.

"I guess this is it," she whispered. "Whatever happens after we walk through that front door will affect my relationship with my parents forever."

Kellan squeezed her hand as the SUV bounced along the long gravel driveway toward the house. "Yes, it will, but that doesn't mean it will have a negative effect."

After parking the SUV next to the barn, he turned and faced her. Leaning forward, he brushed his lips against hers. "Let's go in there and wish them a Merry Christmas. I'll get the gifts from the trunk." He took the keys from the ignition and climbed from the vehicle.

Anna Mae unfastened her seatbelt and turned toward the door. As she leaned forward to exit the vehicle, a sharp pain radiated through her abdomen and stole her breath. She sucked in short, shallow breaths while gripping the door handle in vain as more fire shot from her lower back through her abdomen.

"Annie!" Kellan rushed around the SUV and pulled the door open, and she let her hands drop into her lap. He cupped her face in his hands, alarm glowing in his eyes. "Should I call nine-one-one?" He fished his cell phone from his pocket.

The pain deadened, and she took a ragged breath. "I think I'm okay."

He narrowed his eyes with suspicion. "I don't get that impression from the expression on your face."

She attempted to stand, and the pain flared. "Oh." She sat back in the seat, and the pain moved through her back. She ran her fingers up and down her lower back, which felt like it had been kicked by steel-toed boots. "Maybe I should wait a minute."

"Anna Mae!" a familiar voice called. "Are you going to come in or sit in the car all afternoon while the snow gets worse?"

Anna Mae glanced over at Kathryn hurrying through the snow with a cloak over her purple frock.

"She's having some pain," Kellan said. "I'm concerned she may be going into labor."

"What?" Kathryn's eyes rounded with excitement. "You're in labor?" She took Anna Mae's arm. "Let's get you inside."

Anna Mae swatted her hand away. "No, no. I'm not in labor. I just have some pangs now and then, but nothing regular." She lifted herself from the seat. "Just give me a minute and I can get into the house without any help."

Kellan shook his head. "Don't believe her. She's downplaying the pain I just witnessed. She looked like she was going to pass out from it."

Anna Mae shot Kellan the best serious expression she could conjure despite the dull pain in her abdomen. "I'm fine. Please get the gifts from the trunk and we'll head inside." She took Kathryn's extended arm and they started toward the back door. "I just need to rest when we get inside. I'm sure it's just the excitement of seeing everyone again." She bit her bottom lip. "Do my parents know we're here for lunch?"

"I told your mother." Kathryn smiled. She pulled a shawl from her pocket. "Here. You'd better put this on so that you don't upset your *dat*."

"Good idea." Anna Mae arranged the shawl on her head and tied it under her chin.

Kathryn smiled and hugged her. "I'm so glad you're here."

"*Danki*." Anna Mae held her and sniffed back threatening tears. "I am too."

"Ready?" Kathryn asked with a smile.

"As ready as I'll ever be." Anna Mae glanced back at Kellan. "Shall we go in?"

Holding the shopping bags, he gave a smile. "Absolutely."

Taking a deep breath, Anna Mae followed Kathryn into her parents' home. A rush of memories overcame her as she crossed the threshold. Family gatherings, birthdays, childhood memories flooded her mind and filled her heart with a mixture of happiness and longing for her childhood. She scanned the family room and it looked just as she remembered —an old sofa sat at one wall along with a few arm chairs, end tables, and a coffee table. Keeping with Amish tradition, the Christmas decorations included poinsettias on the mantel over a crackling fire along with a few decorative candles.

Kathryn took Anna Mae's hand and led her to an easy chair, where Anna Mae sat. Kellan sank down in a chair beside her and helped her hand out the candies and little toys she'd brought for her nieces and nephews, who rushed over to greet them.

Anna Mae was talking with Ruthie and Lizzie when she felt eyes studying her. Glancing up, she found her mother, tears spilling from her eyes, standing in the doorway to the kitchen watching her. Her father stood behind her, his eyes cold and his mouth creased in a deep frown. He gave her a hard stare and then disappeared back into the kitchen.

Anna Mae started to stand, but the ache in her back caused her to sink back into the chair.

"Don't get up," Mary Rose said. "I'll come to you." She held her hands out, and Anna Mae took them. "I'm so glad you're here, *Dochder.*"

"Me too." Anna Mae smiled.

"Join us for Christmas Eve dinner, Anna Mae," Mary Rose said. She helped Anna Mae to her feet and steered her toward the kitchen with Kathryn in tow.

Stepping into the kitchen Anna Mae found her father sitting at the table next to David. When he met her gaze, he still frowned and looked away, causing her stomach to plummet. She turned to Kathryn, who gave a dismissive gesture as if reading her mind.

"Sit here," Kathryn said, pointing to a small table next to the larger table in the center of the room. "I'll sit with you."

"I will too," Mary Rose said.

Anna Mae's eyes widened with shock. "You'll sit with me?"

"Of course I will." Mary Rose's voice was confident. "You're my *dochder.*" She patted the chair. "Have a seat, *mei liewe*, and Kathryn, the girls, and I will serve the meal."

"*Danki.*" Anna Mae sank into a chair with Kellan beside her. She glanced over at her father and found him still glowering. He shot her mother a glare, but her mother continued helping Kathryn, Amanda, Ruthie, and Lizzie serve the traditional Amish Christmas meal, including chicken with stuffing, mashed potatoes, gravy, succotash, applesauce, buttered noodles, macaroni and cheese, salad, and pickles.

The delicious smells brought back happy Christmas memories and also caused Anna Mae's mouth to water.

Kellan took her hand and leaned close. "Have you had any more pain?" he whispered.

"No, not really," Anna Mae replied. She'd had some, but she didn't want to mention it to Kellan now. He'd just worry. And she longed to soak up the presence of her family, especially her mother.

During lunch, Kathryn, Amanda, and Mary Rose joined Anna Mae and Kellan, while the rest of David's family and Anna Mae's father sat at the kitchen table.

Anna Mae chatted during the meal, sharing stories of her life in Baltimore and enjoying the stories that Mary Rose, Kathryn, and Amanda told. She frequently looked over at her father, who would scowl and look away. David gave uncomfortable glances toward Anna Mae's table and looked as if he were straining to make conversation with his father, who wasn't responding much at all. However, Anna Mae tried in vain to smile and ignore the ache seeping through her lower back.

After they finished the meal, Mary Rose, Kathryn, and the girls cleared the dishes.

"For dessert we have fruit cake, shoo-fly pie, and butterscotch pudding," Kathryn said as she filled the sink with soapy water. "I thought we'd save them for later on since we enjoyed such a big meal."

"That sounds *gut*," Mary Rose said, gathering the dirty glasses.

While the boys and David left the table, Anna Mae sat with Kellan and watched her father exit the kitchen. The sight of his leaving without speaking to her sent anger and regret tangling within her belly.

The silence between her and her father was nearly as painful as the aching in her lower back. She had to make . things right. She couldn't let her father treat her this way. Life was too short, and her child had a right to know his or her grandparents.

Now was the time to make things right with her father.

She hoisted herself from the chair and sucked in a breath when pain sliced through her abdomen.

"Annie?" Kellan rose and took her hand in his.

"I'm fine," she whispered, starting for the door.

He followed her. "Where are you going?"

"I can't take it anymore. I have to go talk to him." She passed David and the boys and started toward the back door, where she'd seen her father head. She assumed he had retreated to the barn, his favorite place to read his Bible and think. David opened his mouth to speak to her, but Anna Mae continued past him.

"What good will it do?" Kellan asked.

When she didn't respond, he took her arm and gently turned her toward him. "Annie, please answer me. I'm worried about you. You look really upset. Won't talking to your father just make it worse?"

Her voice trembled. "I can't stand the way he's ignoring me." She absently rubbed her back where the pain sizzled. "I need to work this out with him. I have to do it before we go home. If I don't, then I'll regret it for the rest of my life,

Kellan." She touched his cheek. "Don't you understand that? He's my dad, the only dad I'll ever have, and the only living grandfather our child will have."

Frowning, Kellan sighed. "You're not going to let this go, are you?"

"No." She sniffed and wiped her eyes.

"Okay, then we'll make a deal. I'll give you five minutes with him." He snatched her cloak from the peg on the wall by the door and draped it over her shoulders. "If you're not back in five, then I'm coming to get you. Understand?"

She nodded, hugging her cloak to her body. "Thank you."

She gripped the doorknob and trekked out into the blowing snow, stumbling twice on her way to barn. The large, fluffy flakes drenched her cloak and clung to her shawl.

Wrenching open the barn door, Anna Mae trudged into the barn, passing the horse stalls on her way to her father's workshop. The aroma of animals and leather seeped into her senses.

She spotted her father in the corner, sitting on a bench and reading the Bible. She stood in the doorway and studied him for a moment, her body trembling as the pain in her lower back increased anew. She leaned against the door frame and took a deep breath.

"*Daed*," she began, her voice small like a little girl. "*Daed*," she repeated with more force.

He looked up at her and his eyes narrowed before cutting back to the Bible.

"*Daed*, I have something I need to say." She kneaded her lower back with her fingers, hoping to curb some of the discomfort.

He continued reading without acknowledging her. She shivered, absently wondering if the cold was from the temperature of the air in the barn or from his treatment of her.

"Kellan and I came all this way to spend *Grischtdaag* with you, *Mamm*, and everyone else because we want to be a part of the family," she said. "While I made my choice to build a life with Kellan, I never chose to lose you. I'm still a Beiler by birth, and my child is also a Beiler. You can punish me for not staying Amish, but it's unfair to punish my innocent *boppli*."

Her body continued to shake, and the pain from her lower back slithered to her abdomen. She gripped the door frame for balance and took a deep breath.

Her father kept his eyes trained on the Bible.

"Are you going to even look at me?" she asked, her voice small and quiet, squelched by the pain moving down her legs. "I'm a person. I deserve a response."

He met her gaze and scowled. "You've said your piece. Now you may leave."

"That's it?" She shook her head in disbelief as angry tears splattered her cheeks. "I came out here in the blizzard to talk to you and all you can do is dismiss me?"

He stood. "If you won't leave, then I will." He moved past her and marched out of the barn.

Anna Mae covered her face with her hands and sobbed, the pain increasing in her back and abdomen. A few moments later, she heard Kellan calling her name.

"Annie?" Kellan's panicked voice echoed through the barn. "Where are you?"

Anna Mae wiped her eyes. "I'm back here," she said. "By the workshop."

Kellan jogged toward her. "What's going on? I saw your dad come back into the house."

Sobs stole her voice.

He pulled her into his arms. "Are you all right?"

She buried her face in his chest as her tears fell. He rubbed her back.

"That's it," he said. "We're leaving. Now." He took her hand and led her through the snow toward the SUV. "I'll go in to let Kathryn know we're going. You can call her at the bakery next week."

"No." She shook her head. "I want to say goodbye to them."

Pulling the keys from his coat pocket, he hit the unlock button. "You get in the truck, and I'll go get them."

"But—"

He opened the passenger door and gestured for her to climb in. "Please, Annie. It will be easier that way. You can say goodbye and then we'll go to the bed and breakfast and check out." His eyes softened. "You don't need this nonsense from your dad. We can spend Christmas Day at home tomorrow and put this mess behind us." He nodded toward her belly. "We have plenty of good things to look forward to, and that man is not going to steal our joy."

She sighed with defeat and climbed into the car, and he jogged through the blowing snow into the house.

Kellan marched into the house, rage roaring through his veins.

David glanced over from where he stood with Kathryn and Mary Rose, and his eyes widened. "What's wrong?"

"We're leaving," Kellan said. He jammed his thumb toward the door. "Anna's in the car already. Henry upset her, so we're leaving now. You can go say goodbye to Anna Mae. I need to speak with Mr. Beiler."

Kathryn and Mary Rose exchanged surprised expressions and then rushed out the front door.

"Where's your father?" Kellan asked David.

"In the kitchen." David followed him to the doorway.

Kellan found Henry standing with a glass of water in his hands.

"Mr. Beiler," Kellan began. "I'd like to have word with you, man to man, in private."

Henry placed his glass on the counter and gave Kellan a cold look. "Follow me to the porch."

Kellan ignored David's shocked expression and walked with Henry to the enclosed porch, shutting the door behind them.

"What's this about?" Henry asked, standing by the row of windows with his arms folded across his chest.

"You've won," Kellan said. "We're leaving."

"I'm sorry to hear that," Henry said, his voice flat, devoid of emotion. "I pray that God blesses you with a safe trip home."

Kellan shook his head and threw his hands up. "I don't understand you people at all. You claim to be pious Christians, but you're nothing but a hypocrite."

Henry shook his head. "I claim to be nothing. We're all sinners and can only be saved through Christ's grace. We Amish don't think we're better than anyone else. We all are working toward our ultimate salvation. Only God knows what's in your heart and if you've lived a life that's worthy of salvation."

"If you claim that you don't judge others, then why do you treat your sweet Anna Mae like garbage when she comes to visit you?" Kellan demanded, his voice trembling with swelling anger. "How can you consider that a Christian act that will get you salvation?"

Henry glared at him. "You have no right to judge me."

"But you're judging her!" Kellan shook his head. "You've got a lot to learn about what it takes to be a Christian. Your daughter is out in the car nursing a broken heart because of the way *you've* treated her. She thinks you hate her, and from the way you've acted, I'm not certain she's wrong. You need to rethink your role as bishop because I wouldn't go to any service that you led. In fact, I don't know how you sleep at night, Henry Beiler." Kellan turned to leave.

"You're wrong," Henry said, his voice soft. "I don't hate my daughter."

"Really?" Kellan gave a sarcastic snort as he faced him. "You've got a real backward way of showing your love." He paused. "I may not be Amish, but I know what it means to be a Christian," he continued, jamming a finger in his own chest. "I live my life for the glory of God, I love my wife, and I want to raise children who will worship God too. I also know how to show my family that I love them."

Henry stared at him, his expression softening.

"I'll leave you with one thought, Mr. Beiler," Kellan said. "You have a daughter and a future grandchild who may never know you or care to know you. How does that make you feel?"

Turning, Kellan headed back out to the family room, where David stood with an uncomfortable expression. "We're leaving. I'll be in touch." Without waiting for a response, Kellan hurried past the children standing in the family room and out the door to the car. He breathed in a ragged breath hoping to calm his trembling body. A weight had lifted from his shoulders; he'd finally told Henry Beiler what he thought of his hypocritical ways. Now he could focus on what was important: getting his precious Anna Mae home where she belonged.

CHAPTER 11

While she waited in the car, Anna Mae stared out the windshield and took deep breaths. The pain continued to swell, and she bit her bottom lip. She wondered if she should ask Kellan to take her to Lancaster General. However, the pain her father caused in her heart was more overwhelming. She longed to go home and curl up on the sofa in front of the fireplace. Kellan was right: they needed to put this behind them before the baby came. All that mattered was their love, not what her father thought of them.

Coming here was a mistake.

Why did she ever believe her father would accept her?

I'm such a fool to think I can still be considered a part of the family without being Amish.

The door creaked open, and Mary Rose leaned in and hugged her. "I wish you would stay," she whispered. "I hate that you have to leave like this." She held on for several minutes, and Anna Mae hoped she wouldn't cry.

Sniffing, Anna Mae forced a smile. "Maybe we'll come back again someday."

"Or maybe you can come with David and me when we visit in the spring," Kathryn said.

"I would love that," Mary Rose said. *"Ich liebe dich, mei liewe."*

"I love you too, *Mamm.*" Anna Mae squeezed her hand. "Write me."

Mary Rose stepped back, and Kathryn moved to the car and hugged her. "You be safe. It's snowing pretty badly." Kathryn kissed her head. "Call me. I'll be at the bakery on Monday. Love you."

"Love you too." Anna Mae sucked in a breath as more pain flared in her back.

"Was iss letz?" Mary Rose asked, concern flashing in her eyes.

"Nothing." Anna Mae tried to force a smile, but her lips formed a grimace. "You get back inside. It's bitter cold, and the snow is soaking your cloaks." She squeezed their hands. "I love you both. I'll write you as soon as we get home."

Kellan loped over to the car, his expression serious as if he was pondering something.

Kathryn and Mary Rose both hugged Kellan before hurrying back through the snow. Kellan climbed into the driver's seat and jammed the key into the ignition, bringing the SUV to life.

Anna Mae turned her head and watched her mother and Kathryn disappear into the house while fresh tears filled her eyes. She hoped she would see them again soon under better circumstances.

As the truck eased down the driveway toward the road, Anna Mae sucked in a breath. She rubbed her belly with one hand and her back with the other. The sky was pure white, and the large, fluffy flakes kept the windshield wipers working non-stop, *sshhing* back and forth but never making any progress keeping the windshield clear before another batch of snowflakes caked the glass.

Driving in silence, Kellan steered onto the road and the SUV slid sideways. He eased off the gas and slowly continued down the road.

They drove in silence for several miles, and Anna Mae closed her eyes, praying that the pain would subside. However, it increased, and she began to wonder if she was in labor. She opened her mouth to speak, but no words formed. Turning to Kellan, she found his eyes trained on the road, deep in thought.

"When your mom gave me a hug, she whispered in my ear that I should take good care of you," Kellan said, flipping on the defroster. "I find it truly amazing that your mom is so focused on you and so willing to accept you in her life, but your dad is all about the rules. Was he always like that when you were growing up? Was he ever warm to you?"

Anna Mae took short, ragged breaths as more pain surged through her. Suddenly, she felt wetness between her legs, and she gasped.

"Annie?" Kellan jammed on the brakes, and the SUV slid sideways down the road, slamming into a snowbank, throwing Anna Mae forward in the seat.

"Oh no," he said. "This can't be happening. Not now." He put the SUV in reverse, spinning the tires. The vehicle didn't move. Muttering under his breath, he tried again, then he turned to her. "I'm sorry, honey, but we're stuck." He unfastened his seatbelt and leaned over her. "Annie? Are you all right?"

Anna Mae shook her head, tears streaming down her cheeks. "I think my water just broke, and I'm in pain," she whispered. "Horrible pain. You were right. I guess we should've gone to the hospital earlier, but I—" She slammed her eyes shut as another contraction gripped her, stealing her voice.

"Oh, no." Kellan took her hand and she squeezed it with all her might. "Oh, Annie. I'm so sorry. This is a nightmare."

Once the contraction stopped she opened her eyes and breathed in and out slowly. "I need to get to the hospital. Kellan, I think I'm really in labor. I need a doctor now."

He fished his phone from his pocket. Holding it up, he groaned. "No! Not now!" He waved it around, reading the screen. "Stupid cell phone. I thought this company had the best network."

He turned back to her. "You stay in the car. I'm going to see if I can get a signal outside. If not, then I'm going to start banging on doors and get you some help."

"Be careful," she mumbled, sinking back into the seat.

As Kellan climbed from the car, Anna Mae closed her eyes and rubbed her belly, praying that God would grant her a safe delivery for her precious baby.

After they returned to the house, Kathryn followed Mary Rose into the kitchen. "Can I speak with you alone?" she asked.

"*Ya.*" Mary Rose wiped her eyes. "Let's go into the pantry."

Once in the pantry, Kathryn shut the door. "I can't believe Anna Mae left."

"I wish she'd stayed." Mary Rose sniffed. "I feel terrible that it ended so quickly. Last night I prayed that I'd get some time to really visit with her. I even dreamed about it."

"Kellan said Henry really upset her." Kathryn shook her head. "I'd hoped for better. I thought that God would open Henry's heart and mind and inspire him to accept Anna Mae and Kellan's life."

Mary Rose sighed. "*Ya*, me too. But Henry is still the same stubborn old man he was yesterday." She wiped her eyes. "It was like a cruel prank that I spent less than a day with her after all this time. We should've had at least a few days."

"I know." Kathryn gave a sad smile.

"But maybe we can go visit her in the spring. I'd love to see my new *kinskind*." Mary Rose smiled.

Kathryn frowned. "I have a bad feeling that they shouldn't have driven out into that blizzard. The snow is blowing very heavily. When I glanced out the window in the living room, I couldn't see the trees down by the road."

Mary Rose nodded, her eyes brimming with fresh tears. "I agree. It's too dangerous to be on the road. I'm going to worry all night about them."

"I think she may be in labor too." Kathryn folded her arms. "She said she was having back pain and that's what I had with Amanda. My back hurt so badly that it was as if our horse had kicked me."

Mary Rose gasped and cupped her hand to her mouth. "Oh no. I never thought of that. This could be bad."

"I didn't mean to upset you." Kathryn took Mary Rose's hand in her hands. "But I can't shake the feeling that she may need to get to a doctor. I feel like we should do something to help them."

"You're right." Mary Rose nodded. "But what can we do?"

Kathryn wracked her brain and then snapped her fingers. "David can take me to the phone shanty. I have Kellan's cell phone number. I can give them a call and make sure they're okay."

"That's a great idea." Mary Rose smiled. "You're always thinking."

Kathryn chuckled. "That's what David says. I think too much." She opened the door to the pantry. "I'll go talk to David."

Kathryn located David looking at a book with Ruthie and Lizzie in the enclosed porch. He met her gaze and smiled, and she motioned for him to join her in the doorway.

"I need to talk to you," she said as he approached.

He looked concerned. "*Was iss letz?*"

"I'm worried about Anna Mae and Kellan traveling in the snow." She nodded toward the window, where the snow blew in waves through the trees. She couldn't see beyond the fence around the pasture. "She was in pain and I'm worried she's in labor. I'm afraid they'll wind up stuck somewhere or get in an accident."

Rubbing his beard, he glanced out the window. "It is bad out there. I'm not sure what you want me to do about it, though."

She gripped his arm. "We need to check on them. I have Kellan's cell phone number. We can go to the phone shanty at the corner and call. Maybe we can convince them to come back here and stay the night. It would be safer to leave after the plows have cleared the road." She gave him a pleading look. "Please, David. It would be terrible if something happened to them. I need to know they're okay or I'll go crazy with worry."

He sighed. "You're right. I'll take Junior and go."

"No." She shook her head. "Take me. I need to hear it for myself."

He raised an eyebrow in question. "Are you certain?"

"*Ya.*" She took his hand and pulled him toward the door. "*Kumm.* Let's go before the storm gets any worse." Kathryn pulled David toward the back door and found Mary Rose and Henry standing near it.

Mary Rose wore a deep frown while Henry gave her a hard expression. She grabbed Kathryn's arm. "Are you going to call them?" Her eyes were full of hope.

"*Ya,*" Kathryn said with a nod. "We're hoping we can reach Kellan in time to stop them from leaving. Maybe they'll come back and wait out the storm. If Anna Mae will agree to come back." She looked at Henry, who quickly cut his eyes toward the window.

David fetched his coat from the hook and pulled it on. "We better go before they get too far from the house." He pulled on his gloves and then handed Kathryn her cloak, helping her wrap it around her body. "Do you have Kellan's number on you?"

Kathryn pulled it from her apron pocket. "I stuck it in there when she sent it to me."

David turned to the door. "Let's go."

"Be careful." Mary Rose hugged David and then wrapped

her arms around Kathryn. "I'll be praying for your safe return as well as that of Anna Mae and Kellan."

Mary Rose sucked in a breath as Kathryn and David rushed through the snow to the barn. Turning to Henry, she narrowed her eyes. "I'm disappointed in you."

He kept his eyes trained on the window. "You've made that perfectly clear, especially by spending the night on the sofa."

"How could you let Kathryn go out in that snow with David?" she asked. "You should be the one heading out into that storm to check on our *dochder*."

To her surprise, Henry's expression softened slightly, but he remained silent. He looked at her, and her bottom lip trembled.

"I'm worried about Anna Mae," Mary Rose said. "I think you're afraid too, but you just won't admit it to me."

Henry turned back to the window, and Mary Rose silently prayed that God would protect Anna Mae and Kellan and also work on Henry's heart.

CHAPTER 12

Anna Mae bit her lip and tried in vain to stop the tears spurting from her eyes while the pain increased. She practiced the breathing techniques her Lamaze teacher had preached during their classes, but nothing stopped the intense cramping from stealing her breath.

When the passenger door flew open, hope swelled within her.

"Did you call the paramedics?" she asked, gripping Kellan's cold hand.

His brown hair had patches of wet peppered with snow, and his teeth chattered beneath his bluish lips.

"No." He shivered. "I can't get a signal out here." He nodded across the street. "I found a house over there. You can't see it beyond the snow. I banged on the front door, but there was no answer." His eyes filled with concern. "How are you?"

"I'm in pain. The contractions are getting harder and closer together." Her tears started again. "I'm scared. What should we do? I may deliver here in the car." She glanced out the back window. "How close are we to my *mamm's* house? Maybe we can walk back there and she can help me. She's had five babies of her own and helped to deliver many more." The pain started again, and she sucked in a breath and gripped Kellan's cold hands. Closing her eyes, she tried concentrating on something else, but the cramps burned through her mind and white-hot pain ran through her entire body.

"Annie," he whispered, pushing sweaty wisps of hair back from her face. "Just hold on to me. You're going to be just fine. I promise. Do you want me to count like we did in class? One ... Two ... Three ... Four ... Five ..."

The pain stopped and she leaned back in the seat.

Kellan kissed her hands and then grimaced. "This is all my fault. We should've stayed at the house and just ignored your father. At least then you would've delivered with your mom and Kathryn there to help you."

"Can we get back to the house?" she asked. "Maybe we can walk."

"No." He shook his head and glanced out the window. "I'm afraid something will happen if we try to walk there. I know I can lift you, but I'm not certain I can carry you that far."

"Then I guess we have to stay here until someone comes by," she said, her voice ragged with exhaustion from the pain. "Do you have that roadside safety kit? Can you put the flares out by the car? Maybe then someone would spot us and stop."

"That's a great idea. I'll be right back." He rushed to the back of the vehicle. The trunk opened with a whoosh, and the vehicle rocked back and forth while he rummaged through it.

After several minutes, the trunk slammed shut, and Kellan appeared by the door. "I set out the flares. Let's pray someone comes by and helps us soon."

"I'm sure most people are not going to venture out into

this blizzard," she whispered. "But I pray someone comes by soon or this baby will be born here."

Kellan's countenance became pale. His eyes then flashed with an idea. "I saw a barn over there." He jerked his thumb in the direction of the house. "We should move you there."

"No." She shook her head. "I don't want to go to a barn. I'd rather stay here. The seat is sort of comfortable."

"I think we need to move you." He took her hand. "I'm worried that someone will come along and crash into our car. Let me get the first-aid kit from the trunk and then we'll move you to the barn."

"But the flares," she said. "Why would you set them up and then leave?"

"They'll alert them that we need help," he said. "Someone will see the abandoned truck and know we need help. I can even leave a note."

He pulled a notepad from the glove compartment, and Anna Mae craned her neck to see what he was writing. He scribbled out a fast note, explaining that he had taken his pregnant wife to the barn nearby. He ended the note by asking them to call nine-one-one as soon as possible and get help. Folding the note, he wrote "HELP" across the front and placed it in the driver's side window.

He kissed her forehead. "Trust me, Annie. This will work. Don't move. I'll go get the first-aid kit and a blanket."

He disappeared for a moment and the trunk opened again. It then slammed shut, rocking the truck and causing the pain in her back to ignite. She sucked in a breath and rubbed her abdomen, praying that the discomfort would subside.

He reappeared with the first-aid kit in his hands and a blanket slung over his shoulder. "Ready?" he asked.

"I guess so." She tried to move, but her legs buckled under her. "I need help getting up."

"Hold this." He handed her the first-aid kit. He then reached down and lifted her into his arms, closing the door with his leg. She held onto him while he carried her through the whipping snow and wind. Closing her eyes, she buried her face in his neck. She held her breath and bit down on her lip when the pain swelled again through her back and abdomen.

After several minutes, they reached the large red barn. Kellan gently placed her on her feet and then yanked the door open, grunting and groaning with the effort. They stepped into the large barn, and Anna Mae breathed in the aroma of wet hay and animals. Stables lined the wall, and a horse whinnied in the distance.

"I think I know how Mary felt," she muttered.

Kellan gave a bark of laughter, his handsome face lighting up. He pulled her into his arms. "You are a trooper, Anna Mae."

"Thanks," she said. She then glanced around the large, open space leading to the stalls. "I guess I should sit here." She took the blanket from his shoulder and placed it on the floor.

Slowly, she gingerly sat down, and the hay beneath the blanket gave her little cushion from the cold ground. She looked up at Kellan and opened her mouth to speak, but a sudden, gripping contraction tore through her, leaving her breathless. She rolled onto her side and gasped.

"Annie!" Kellan dropped to his knees and rubbed her back. "Count with me. One, two, three, four, five—"

"Oh," she groaned, tears flowing down her cheeks as she hugged her arms to her chest. "I need my mother. Please, Kellan, go get her for me. I can't do this alone." She turned to him and pleaded with him. "Please, Kellan. Go get her before it's too late. We're not that far from home. You could be there in less than an hour."

Looking confused, he opened his mouth and then closed it again. "But I can't leave you." He took her hands in his and his eyes filled with uncertainty. "What if something happens and I'm not here? What if you need me?"

She squeezed his hands. "If you hurry, I won't be here alone. Besides, most women are in labor for hours and hours before they deliver, especially when it's their first baby." She pointed toward the door. "Go and hurry back."

He leaned down and brushed his lips across hers. He then stared at her, his eyes full of intensity. "I'll hurry back as quickly as I can."

"Thank you." She gritted her teeth as another pang hit her and Kellan disappeared out the barn door. Closing her eyes, she prayed that she wouldn't be forced to deliver her baby alone.

Kathryn shivered while she ran through the swirling snow-flakes to the phone shanty, which was located on the corner between her mother-in-law's home and the neighboring farm. The shanty, which Mary Rose shared with her neighbor, was a small shed containing a phone, stool, and phonebook. Her heart pounded in her chest as she pulled out the phone number scribbled on the piece of paper. She lifted the receiver and punched in the number.

Cradling the receiver between her neck and shoulder, she glanced back at David standing in the doorway. He rubbed his gloved hands together and shivered.

Instead of a ring, a recorded voice sounded through the receiver, saying, "We're sorry. The wireless customer you are trying to reach is not available."

"Oh no," she groaned. "It sounds like Kellan's phone isn't on or it isn't able to find a signal."

"Call the bed and breakfast," David said. "See if they've arrived for their luggage."

"Good idea." Kathryn quickly looked up the number in the phonebook. Sandra Sheppard answered and said no, she hadn't seen Kellan or Anna Mae since they left.

With a sigh, Kathryn replaced the receiver and glanced at David. "No sign of them at the bed and breakfast. If they haven't arrived back there yet, then they're probably in trouble. It's been nearly an hour since they left." She glanced past David toward the falling snow. "Hopefully they've stopped nearby."

David shook her head. "Katie, the snow is coming down like crazy and the roads are slick. We're *narrisch* if we try to venture out too far from the house. We may not be able to get back."

"Please." She tugged at his sleeve. "Let's just go a few miles up the road toward the bed and breakfast and then we'll head home. I just have to see if they need help. I can't stop this feeling I have that we need to search for them."

He sighed, glancing toward the direction of the barn. "Let's go hitch up the horse and buggy."

"*Danki.*" She rushed through the snow, holding onto his arm to avoid slipping on the slick snow on the way to the barn.

Once the horse was hitched, she climbed in and covered her legs with a quilt.

David sat beside her and guided the horse down the road. They headed up the long drive and out to the main road, driving in silence for more than twenty minutes.

Kathryn closed her eyes and prayed with all her might that God would lead Anna Mae and Kellan to safety.

"What color is Kellan's car?" David asked, breaking through her silent prayers.

"I think it's burgundy," Kathryn said. She gasped, cupping her gloved hands to her mouth when her eyes found what had caught David's attention. Flares lined an abandoned burgundy SUV that was nosed into a snowbank, snow covering the roof end and part of the hood.

"Oh no," she said. "Where are they, David? Where are Anna Mae and Kellan?"

CHAPTER 13

While trudging through the snow to the street, Kellan silently prayed Anna Mae and the baby would make it through this ordeal safely. He'd never in his wildest thoughts imagined that he would wind up in a blizzard with Anna Mae in labor. He wished he'd listened to his gut and convinced Anna Mae to stay home and not travel this late in her pregnancy.

When he slipped down a snow-covered hump, he knew he'd hit the pavement. He tented his hand over his eyes in an attempt to shield himself from the raging snow. And then he saw it. A horse and buggy!

He threw his hands in the air, waving frantically. The buggy pulled up next to him, and the door opened, revealing David. "Kellan!" David yelled.

"Thank God you're here!" Kellan climbed up the step.

David leaned over. "Where's Annie? Are you all right?"

"We need your help," Kellan gasped, trying to catch his breath. "Annie's in labor."

"Oh no!" Kathryn pushed past David, her blue eyes full of worry. "Where is she?"

Kellan pointed behind him. "I carried her to a barn

because I was worried a passing vehicle might crash into us if we stayed in the SUV. I told her she'd be safer in the barn. I didn't want to leave her there alone, but she begged me to get her mother. Her water broke, and the contractions are getting stronger."

Kathryn leaped from the buggy and grabbed Kellan's arm. "Let's go quickly. I'll help her."

"Wait a minute." David jumped from the buggy and clasped his hand around Kathryn's arm, stopping her mid-gait. "Who's that?" He nodded toward an oncoming buggy.

Kathryn pulled from his grip. "You wait and see. I'm worried about Anna Mae." She turned to Kellan. "Take me to her."

"All right." Kellan extended his arm, and she took it. He then glanced back at David. "We're going straight toward that red barn, just past that house."

David nodded. "I'll come find you after I see who this is. The buggy looks like someone from our district."

Kellan then led Kathryn to the barn, where they found Anna Mae on her side, sobbing.

"Anna Mae!" Kathryn rushed over to her and dropped to her knees. "How close are the contractions? Do you feel like you need to push?"

The women continued their conversation in Pennsylvania Dutch, and Kellan turned toward the entrance to the barn. He stepped over to the door and leaned on the doorway. Pulling his cell phone from his pocket, he held it up, praying he'd find a bar. However, the phone still displayed: "No service." Closing his eyes, he prayed, begging God to get Anna Mae and the baby through this safely.

Approaching voices caused him to open his eyes. His mouth gaped when he found David flanked by Henry and Mary Rose.

When Henry gave Kellan a worried expression, Kellan's gut swelled with hope. Had Kellan gotten through to him? Had the man finally realized how badly he'd treated his youngest daughter?

"How is she?" Mary Rose asked, worry glistening in her eyes.

"I think she's in labor," Kellan said. "Kathryn's with her."

Mary Rose ran toward the two women and joined in their conversation, barking orders in Pennsylvania Dutch.

"Can we move her?" Henry asked.

Kellan folded his arms across his chest and shivered. "I don't know. I would like to get her out of this barn, but my fear is that I'll do something to hurt her and the baby."

"I think it would be wise to take her to the house," Henry said to David.

David nodded. "At least then it would be warm and sanitary." He looked at Kellan. "We can take her in the buggy and come back for the car when the snow lets up."

"*Ya*, I agree," Henry said. "I'll go see what Mary Rose thinks. We may have to get her out of here fast." He moved past Kellan and joined the women.

"How did he know to come here?" Kellan asked David.

David shook his head with confusion. "I'm not sure. He said my *mamm* was really worried about Anna Mae and insisted he go look for her." He grinned. "I don't know what you said to him at the house, but I get the feeling that you may have gotten his attention."

Kellan nodded. "Good. Maybe we're on the road to an apology."

"Don't get too excited yet. He's a stubborn old man."

"We need to move her now," Henry called, motioning for them to move over to Anna Mae.

"I'll carry her," Kellan said, rushing over. "I carried her in here." He turned to Kathryn. "Is she close?"

"I think so." She nodded with emphasis. "It may be soon, like within the next hour. We're only twenty minutes from home. I think we need to try to get her back."

"Let's go now." Kellan lifted her up. "It'll be all right, Annie," he whispered in her ear. "We're going to take good care of you."

She bit down on her lip and nodded, her eyes full of worry and pain.

Mary Rose looked at David. "Take your buggy and go get Vera, Fannie, and Barbie. Ask them to come to the house to help. I need them to help Kathryn and me."

"I will," David said, nodding.

"Hurry!" Mary Rose called after him.

David and Kathryn rushed off to their buggy, and Kellan carried Anna Mae out to Henry's buggy and placed her in the back seat. He rode with her, holding her hand and talking to her, while Henry steered the buggy back to his house.

During the ride, the snow continued to blow, pelting the buggy windshield. The roads were slick, and Kellan worried that emergency crews wouldn't be able to make it out to the house to help Anna Mae.

When they arrived at Mary Rose's house, Kellan carried Anna Mae into Mary Rose's bedroom and placed her on the bed. He kissed her cheek while she clenched her jaw and moaned in pain. He held her hand and brushed her hair back from her face while whispering words of encouragement and love.

Mary Rose entered the room holding several towels. "Your sisters should be here soon," she said, placing the towels on a chair near the bed. "It shouldn't take long to get down the road to their homes. I'm so thankful they live close by." She stood across from Kellan and gave him a hopeful smile. "She'll be just fine."

He nodded, hoping she was right. He continued to hold Anna Mae's hand while Mary Rose rubbed Anna Mae's lower back and muttered words in Pennsylvania Dutch.

Nearly thirty minutes later, Anna Mae's three sisters and Kathryn burst into the room. The sisters gathered around Anna Mae and hugged her, speaking words he couldn't interpret. Speechless, Kellan watched the scene with his eyes wide, wondering what had moved Fannie and Barbie to finally accept Anna Mae. Was it a miracle?

The women then seemed to call out instructions, because Amanda, her sisters, and cousins rushed through the house, bringing supplies to the bedroom, including pitchers of water, towels, and quilts.

While the women tended to Anna Mae, Kellan moved to the enclosed porch. Sitting in a chair, he clasped his hands, bowed his head, closed his eyes, sending up a fervent prayer for Anna Mae and their baby, begging God to keep them healthy and safe during the delivery. He then opened his eyes and held up his phone. When two bars appeared, he shouted for joy.

"Is that phone contraption working?" a voice behind him asked.

Turning, he found Henry standing in the doorway.

"Yes, it's finally picking up a signal," Kellan said. "I couldn't get it to work earlier when we were on the road and Annie took a turn for the worse."

Henry stepped onto the porch. "David told me that. I have to commend you on how you took care of Anna Mae while you were stuck in the snow. Putting out flares and taking her to the barn was very wise."

"Thanks," Kellan said with surprise. "I never expected a compliment from you. It means a lot."

Henry pointed toward the phone. "Are you going to call for help? It sounds like Anna Mae is going to deliver that *boppli* soon, and we'll have to get her to a hospital to be sure she and the *boppli* are okay."

"Yes, I'll call right now." Kellan dialed nine-one-one and explained to the dispatcher that his wife was in labor and needed help right away. When she asked for an address, Kellan gave Henry a blank expression. "I'm sorry, but I can't remember the address here."

Henry held out his hand. "I'll take care of it." Taking the phone, he explained the address and even gave detailed directions. He told the dispatcher that it was a dire emergency and to send help as soon as possible. He snapped the phone shut and handed it to Kellan. "She said it may take awhile due to the storm."

Kellan slipped the phone back into his coat pocket. "Yeah, she told me that too."

"Don't worry." Henry patted his shoulder. "My Mary Rose

has delivered many *bopplin* over the years. My other daughters are experienced as well, and I'm certain they can handle it. Anna Mae is in very good hands and the Lord is good. After all, tomorrow is Christmas Day."

Stunned by Henry's sudden compassion, Kellan nodded.

"The Lord will take care of Anna Mae and her *boppli*." Henry sank into a chair. "You look like you have the weight of the world on your shoulders. I'm certain everything will be just fine. Would you like to sit with me while we wait for news of your *boppli*?"

Kellan sat beside him. He stared at Henry. "Why the change of heart? Is it only because the baby is coming?"

Henry's eyes got a faraway look and he tugged at his beard. "I was wrong to be so harsh with you and Anna Mae. You made me see that."

"My words made you realize that?" Kellan asked.

"*Ya*, you made me to see how badly I've treated you and Anna Mae, and I'm very sorry. I hope you can find it in your heart to forgive me."

Kellan shook his head with disbelief. "Of course I can forgive you. Jesus explicitly commands us to love and forgive each other. I may not be Amish, but I believe in the same God you do and I take His teachings seriously."

"I saw you praying out here." Henry held out his hand, and Kellan shook it. "Thank you for taking such good care of my daughter. I can tell she's very happy with you and her life in Baltimore. I should've thanked you a long time ago."

Kellan smiled. "Thank you for welcoming us back into the family."

David stepped out onto the porch. He looked between

Henry and Kellan and raised his eyebrows with surprise. "It's *gut* to see you both talking."

Henry nodded. "I thought I should get to know my English son-in-law."

David smiled. "Anna Mae made a good decision when she picked Kellan."

"I appreciate that," Kellan said. "I feel blessed to have her for my wife." He glanced back toward the doorway. "Do you think she's doing okay in there? Should I go check on her?"

David shook his head. "The women have it under control. They'll call you if they need you."

Kellan ran his lower lip through his teeth and clasped his hands together. While he'd participated in the Lamaze classes, he'd never felt comfortable with the birthing process. He hoped that the women could handle things until the EMTs arrived.

He turned back to Henry, who was in a deep discussion with David about the storm. Glancing out the window, he found the snow still blowing full force. "When do you think the ambulance will get here?"

"I'm sure they'll get here as soon as they can," Henry said.

Kellan moved to the window. "What if they don't get here in time?"

David placed a hand on Kellan's shoulder. "It will be fine. Four of my five children were born at home without any problems. My *mamm* knows what she's doing. Trust me."

❧

"I can't do it," Anna Mae groaned, squeezing her eyes together while lying in bed. "It's too hard."

Mary Rose chuckled while applying a cold compress to Anna Mae's head. "*Ya,* you can and you will. There's only one way to get this *boppli* out, and he's ready to come." She rubbed Anna Mae's arm. "When the next contraction comes, push from the bottom of your toes, *ya?* You're almost there."

Kathryn leaned over. "*Mamm* is right. I think the *boppli* is almost crowning."

The contraction started and Anna Mae pushed as hard as she could, giving it all of the strength she could muster.

"Push again, Anna Mae!" Mary Rose exclaimed. "I can see the head! It's coming fast."

"I need my husband," Anna Mae said. "Please go get him. He needs to be here to see his baby enter the world."

Kathryn rushed to the door and opened it. "Amanda, go get Kellan! We need him now. It's time!" She then stood by Anna Mae and took her hand.

Anna Mae began to push as another contraction hit. Pressure shot through her lower back. "I can't take it." She sobbed. "It hurts too much. I can't do it!"

"Keep going," Mary Rose said. "It's almost here."

The door opened and then slammed shut as Kellan appeared beside her. His face was pale but his eyes were bright.

"Take her hand," Kathryn said. "I'll step back."

"Come on, Anna Mae," Mary Rose said. "One more push."

"Come on, honey," Kellan said, holding her hand. "You can do it." He leaned down and brushed the cool compress over her forehead. "You're strong. Just one more push."

Anna Mae bore down and gave it all she could. Soon she felt the pressure ease and Mary Rose yelped with joy, holding a tiny bundle in her hands. She and Kathryn cleaned the baby, and, with tears streaming down his cheeks, Kellan cut the cord.

"Is the baby okay?" Anna Mae whispered, her strength depleted.

"Yes, he is." Kellan took her hands in his.

"Did you say *he*?" Anna Mae asked.

"I did." He brushed back her hair. "It's a boy, Annie. We have a son."

"A Christmas Eve miracle," Mary Rose said, placing the bundle in Anna Mae's arms.

Anna Mae stared down into the eyes of her newborn child and then glanced up at Kellan. "Merry Christmas, Kellan."

"Merry Christmas to you." He kissed her lips.

Epilogue

Anna Mae hummed while gazing down at her sleeping infant. Leaning back in the hospital bed, she sighed. Life was pretty close to perfect. It was Christmas Day, and she was in Lancaster General Hospital holding her newborn son.

Anna Mae, the baby, and Kellan had arrived at the hospital late last night. Since only immediate family members were allowed to ride in the ambulance, the rest of her family had stayed behind, promising to visit after the plows had come through and cleared the roads.

After reaching the hospital, Anna Mae was admitted, and the baby was whisked away for tests. He passed them all with flying colors and was declared perfectly healthy. The three of them had spent the night in Anna Mae's room. However, Anna Mae had hardly slept. She'd spent most of the night staring at her baby boy, marveling at how perfect he was and how much God had blessed her.

The door squeaked open, revealing Kellan holding a tray containing two large Styrofoam drink cups and some snacks from the cafeteria. "I got you sweet tea and a blueberry muffin."

"Thank you," Anna Mae said with a smile. She nodded

toward the baby. "He's sleeping. Isn't he beautiful? I can't believe he's ours."

Kellan placed the tray on the bedside table and leaned over her. "Believe it because it's true." He brushed his lips across hers. "Merry Christmas, Annie. I love you."

"Merry Christmas," she echoed. "I love you too."

"You gave me the best gift of all, our son." He reached over and ran a fingertip down the baby's cheek.

"No, I didn't. God did." She kissed the baby's forehead. "Now we need to figure out the biggest question of all: What will we name him? We never agreed on a boy's name. You said you didn't like Kellan Junior."

"You're right; I still don't like it. However, the name quandary is going to have to wait." Kellan stood up straight. "There is a group of visitors outside anxious to see you and the baby. Would it be okay if I let them come in?"

"My family? They're here." Anna Mae grimaced. "Oh no. I haven't showered yet. I'm a mess."

"You look beautiful as always." Kellan kissed her forehead. "Should I let them in?"

"I guess so." She took a deep breath. "I'm ready."

Kellan disappeared out the door and then entered followed by Kathryn, David, Amanda, and her parents.

Anna Mae sat up straighter, her eyes trained on her father's smile. Her heart pounded against her ribcage. Had her father had a change of heart? If so, then this was a bigger Christmas miracle than the baby!

"Congratulations!" Amanda rushed over to the bed with Kathryn close behind her. "He's my cutest cousin."

"He's even more beautiful today than last night." Kathryn

touched the blanket wrapped around his tiny body. "Have you chosen a name yet?"

Anna Mae glanced at Kellan. He shrugged while sitting in a chair by the window.

"No, we haven't agreed yet," Anna Mae said.

"You need a good strong name for that handsome fellow," Mary Rose said, standing next to Kathryn. "He's exquisite."

"*Danki*," Anna Mae whispered, staring down at him. "I was just telling Kellan that I can't believe this beautiful little bundle is mine."

"You mean ours," Kellan said with a chuckle.

"Right, that's what I meant." Anna Mae gazed up at David.

"Congratulations, *schweschder*," he said. "He's *schee*. May God bless you with many more."

Anna Mae laughed. "*Danki*, David. I don't think I'm in any hurry, though."

"May I hold him?" Mary Rose held out her hands.

"Of course." Anna Mae lifted the baby, and Mary Rose took him.

Kellan stood and motioned for Mary Rose to sit in his chair. She sank down and began to talk to the baby while rubbing his chin.

Anna Mae looked at her *daed* standing at the end of the bed. "Hi," she said.

"Hello," Henry said, absently fingering the brim of his hat in his hands. "How are you feeling?"

"Fine," she said, smoothing the sheet over her legs. "I'm a little sore, but it's not too bad. I'm taking some good pills." She studied his eyes. "It's good to see you."

He nodded. "*Frehlicher Grischtdaag.*"

"*Frehlicher Grischtdaag* to you too." She gave Kellan a sideways glance and found him smiling as if he knew something she didn't. She made a mental note to ask him about that later.

"I wanted to apologize," Henry said. "I'm sorry for treating you so badly. I was very wrong."

Anna Mae sniffed and wiped her eyes that had suddenly filled with tears. "*Danki* for telling me that. You're my *daed* and my son's only *grossdaddi*. We need you, *Dat*."

Moving around the bed, Henry took her hand and kissed it. "Welcome home, *dochder*."

She wiped tears from her cheeks with her free hand. "What caused you to change your mind about Kellan and me?"

Henry nodded toward Kellan, who was still smiling. "Your husband had a talk with me. He told me my actions were not Christian."

Anna Mae gasped. "Kellan told you that?"

"*Ya*, that's right," Henry said, absently turning the brim of his hat in his hands. "Although you didn't pick an Amish man, you chose a man who loves God and takes *gut* care of you."

"*Danki, Daed*." Anna Mae opened her arms, and he gave her a quick, gentle hug. "*Ich liebe dich, Daed*."

"*Ich liebe dich*, Anna Mae," he said, his voice raspy with emotion. Standing up, he wiped tears from his eyes. "I hope you will come often," he said. "I'll want to get to know my grandson."

"I thought we would all go visit Anna Mae and Kellan in the spring," David said, standing by Kathryn.

Her father smiled. "That sounds *gut*." He turned to Kellan. "If you'll welcome us into your home."

Kellan smiled. "Of course we will. You're family."

"Another Christmas miracle," Mary Rose whispered, her voice thick. "First, this beautiful baby, and now our family is back together."

"God is *gut*," David said.

"*Ya*, he is," Kathryn chimed in.

❧

Later that afternoon, Kathryn held David's hand as they crossed the snowy parking lot toward the waiting car. She breathed in the crisp air and smiled.

"It truly feels like *Grischtdaag* when there's snow on the ground," she said, smiling up at him. "Those warm Christmases we had for a few years didn't feel authentic."

He nodded. "You know, I haven't thanked you yet."

"Thanked me?" She stopped and studied his eyes.

"I need to thank you for making this the best *Grischtdaag* ever."

She tilted her head in question. "What do you mean?"

"You managed to bring my family back together," he said. "*Danki*."

"Wait a minute." She took his hand, stopping him in midstride. "So, you're saying that I was right to invite Anna Mae here?"

He grinned. "*Ya*, you were."

She raised her eyebrows. "And I was right that it was a sign from God?"

"Maybe so. I'm sorry for doubting you, Katie. Your best

intentions turned out the way you'd planned. You even changed my father's heart." Leaning down he brushed his lips across hers. "You worked the most *wunderbaar* miracle I've ever seen."

She wrapped her arms around his neck. "I can't take credit for it. It was all God. I just asked Him to use me as He saw fit."

"Then I should say *danki* for listening to God when He inspired you to bring my sister here." He hugged her. "*Iche liebe dich, mei liewe. Frehlicher Grischtdaag.*"

"*Ich liebe dich*, David," she whispered in his ear. "*Frehlicher Grischtdaag* to you too."

Later that evening, Anna Mae held the baby close and ran her fingertip down his warm cheek, causing him to sigh in his sleep. "I think he looks like you."

"How can you tell?" Kellan leaned over her. "He's so tiny."

"Yes, but he has your cute little nose." She grinned up at him. "He's going to be a ladies' man like you."

Kellan laughed. "Right, me a ladies' man." He rubbed her shoulder. "Have you given a name any thought?"

"How about Aidan Beiler McDonough?"

"Hmm," he rubbed his chin. "That's not half bad. I think I like it."

"Aidan in memory of your dad and Beiler in honor of my family and our wonderful trip here." She stared down at the sleeping baby. "What do you think, Aidan? Is it a good name?"

"I think it's perfect." Kellan kissed her cheek. "Aidan Beiler McDonough it is."

Glancing at him, Anna Mae smiled. "Thank you for bringing me here. This has been the most wonderful Christmas ever."

He raised an eyebrow. "You'd rank getting stuck in a snowbank and nearly giving birth in a barn as a good Christmas?"

She nodded. "Yes, because I spent it with you and our baby boy. And I got my family back. Thank you for making my dreams come true."

"You're welcome." He kissed her lips and then grinned. "Can you promise me that next Christmas we'll spend a few quiet days at home in front of a warm fire?"

Anna Mae chuckled. "Yes, I can promise you that."

"Thank you." He brushed his lips against hers. "Merry Christmas, Annie."

"Merry Christmas, Kellan." She glanced down at the baby. "And merry first Christmas, Aidan."

Kauffman Amish Bakery Fruit Cake

1½ cups sugar
2 eggs
2 cups applesauce or
    2 cups fruit (any kind)
½ cup oil
2 cups flour
¼ tsp salt
2 tsp baking soda

Mix together all ingredients and pour into a greased 9 x 13 pan. Bake at 350 degrees for 45 minutes.

Icing

1 stick butter
½ cup evaporated milk
¾ cup brown sugar
1 tsp vanilla

Stir together in a saucepan, then boil 5 minutes. Cool cake and cover with icing.

Discussion Questions

1. Take a walk in Anna Mae's shoes. Would you have dealt with her family problems differently?

2. Kathryn goes against her husband's wishes when she helps Anna Mae plan her trip to Lancaster. While she's following her heart, she's also deceiving David and risking his trust. Have you ever done something you felt was right at the risk of hurting someone you love? If so, how did the situation turn out in the end? Share this with the group.

3. Throughout the story, characters quote Colossians 3:13: "Bear with each other and forgive whatever grievances you may have against one another. Forgive as the Lord forgave you." What does this verse mean to you?

4. David finds himself caught in the middle between Anna Mae and his father. Have you ever found yourself in the role of peacemaker due to a family, social, or work situation? If so, how did you handle the conflict? Did it turn out the way you'd hoped? Share this with the group.

5. When Anna Mae first returns to Lancaster County, she tries to reconcile with her father, only to have him shut her out again. Think of a time when you felt lost and alone. Where did you find your strength? What Bible verses would help with this?

6. Which character can you identify with the most? Which character seemed to carry the most emotional stake in the story? Was it Anna Mae, Kellan, Mary Rose, Henry, Kathryn, or David?

7. We learn that Henry Beiler feels hurt and rejected that Anna Mae left the community. While he is the bishop and preaches about forgiveness, he has a difficult time forgiving her for breaking his heart. Have you ever felt hurt or rejected by a member of your family? How did you come to terms with that hurt? Did you forgive the person who hurt you? Share this with the group if you're comfortable.

8. Kellan confronts Henry about his treatment of his daughter. Have you ever had to confront someone about their bad or hurtful actions? Share this with the group.

9. Mary Rose is convicted by Ephesians 4:2: "Be completely humble and gentle; be patient, bearing with one another in love." What does this verse mean to you?

10. What did you learn about Amish holiday traditions? What is your opinion of their customs? Should we, as non-Amish, adopt more of their traditions of making Christmas more religious and less commercial? Share your thoughts with the group.

Acknowledgments

To my best friend and mother, Lola Goebelbecker. Thank you for your love, support, and encouragement. You're the best plotting partner ever!

My husband, Joe, and our sons, Zac and Matt, you are my life. I love you. Thank you for tolerating my endless hours with my MacBook glued to my lap and my eyes trained on the screen.

I'm grateful to my mother-in-law, Sharon Clipston, for her love and support. Thank you for sharing my books with friends and family members and for telling every bookstore manager in Hampton Roads to order more copies.

I'm so blessed to have my patient friends who critique and edit for me—Sue McKlveen, Margaret Halpin, and Lauran Rodriguez. Thank you for your loyal friendship and helpful critiques! Thank you for always dropping everything to do last-minute proofreading and offer suggestions to make the story stronger.

Thank you to my special Amish friends who patiently answer my endless stream of questions.

I send my sincerest appreciation to my agent Mary Sue Seymour for her professional expertise and friendship.

I'm more grateful than words can express to the Zondervan team. Thank you to my amazing editors — Sue Brower and Becky Philpott. I'm so blessed to be a part of the Zondervan family. Special thanks to Lori Vanden Bosch for editing this book and helping make the story much stronger.

To my readers — thank you for choosing my books. I also enjoy your emails and Facebook conversations.

Thank you most of all to God for giving me the inspiration and the words to glorify You. I'm so thankful and humbled You've chosen this path for me.

Share Your Thoughts

With the Author: Your comments will be forwarded to
the author when you send them to *zauthor@zondervan.com*.

With Zondervan: Submit your review of this book
by writing to *zreview@zondervan.com*.

Free Online Resources at
www.zondervan.com

Zondervan AuthorTracker: Be notified whenever your favorite
authors publish new books, go on tour, or post an update
about what's happening in their lives at www.zondervan.com/
authortracker.

Daily Bible Verses and Devotions: Enrich your life with daily
Bible verses or devotions that help you start every morning
focused on God. Visit www.zondervan.com/newsletters.

Free Email Publications: Sign up for newsletters on Christian
living, academic resources, church ministry, fiction, children's
resources, and more. Visit www.zondervan.com/newsletters.

Zondervan Bible Search: Find and compare Bible passages in
a variety of translations at www.zondervanbiblesearch.com.

Other Benefits: Register yourself to receive online benefits
like coupons and special offers, or to participate in research.

ZONDERVAN®

ZONDERVAN.com/
AUTHORTRACKER
follow your favorite authors